I0646902

FLAMES

BOOK TWO OF THE GALAXY ON FIRE SERIES

CRAIG ROBERTSON

FLAMES

BOOK TWO OF THE *GALAXY ON FIRE SERIES*

by Craig Robertson

IF YOU CAN'T BE DEAD, MAKE SURE THEY
NOTICE YOU

Imagine-It Publishing
El Dorado Hills, CA

ALSO BY CRAIG ROBERTSON:

* Podium Entertainment has produced audiobooks for all the below titles except the older standalone books.

For specifics as to the correct order for reading the Ryanverse, click here.

BOOKS IN THE RYANVERSE:

THE FOREVER SERIES (2016)

THE FOREVER LIFE, Book 1

THE FOREVER ENEMY, Book 2

THE FOREVER FIGHT, Book 3

THE FOREVER QUEST, Book 4

THE FOREVER ALLIANCE, Book 5

THE FOREVER PEACE, Book 6

THE FOREVER BOXSET, Part 1, Books 1 & 2

THE FOREVER BOXSET, Part 2, Book 3 & 4

THE FOREVER BOXSET, Part 3, Book 5 & 6

GALAXY ON FIRE SERIES (2017)

EMBERS, Book 1

FLAMES, Book 2

FIRESTORM, Book 3

FIRES OF HELL, Book 4

DRAGON FIRE, Book 5

For more information about Craig, his books, various series, or to see images and videos for some of his wild alien characters, please visit his website. You'll be glad you did: https://craigarobertson.com/

To sign up for Craig's newsletter to get announcements, updates, and his recommendations for other great Sci-Fi reads go to: https://preview.mailerlite.io/forms/2369493/188634426375144501/share

Copyright 2018 Craig Robertson

All rights reserved. No part of this book may be reproduced or utilized in any form or by any means, electronic or mechanical, including photocopying, recording, or by any information storage or retrieval system without written permission from the author.

ISBN: 978-0-9989253-3-2 (E-Book)
978-0-9989253-4-9 (Paperback)
979-8-7754060-4-2 (Hardcover)

Cover design by Jessica Bell

Formatting services by Drew Avera
drewavera@gmail.com

Editors: Michael R. Blanche
Neil Farr

First Edition 2018
Second Edition 2019
Third Edition 2020

This book is dedicated to my magical, loving, beautiful wife Karen. Thanks for being my best friend. Love you always.

ACKNOWLEDGMENTS

I want to specifically thank my fastest, best, and most loyal beta readers. Here's to you Charles Pitts, Tony Hall, and Jeff Worthen. Seriously, dudes, I couldn't have done it without you!

Note: Glossary of Terms Is Located at the End of the Book

ONE

Two Adamant walked into a dark open room located far underground. The lead one was obese by Adamant standards, which were extremely strict. He wore a dingy enlisted's uniform, covered by a thick black plastic apron that tied over his back. The apron glistened with blood and other less-identifiable specks. The officer, following at a noticeable distance, had the very picture of disgust and disdain on his pinched face.

"Why is it necessary for me to be in this revolting place, Packlet Minor Feltopia?" Grand Inquisitor Heldogra asked, as he covered his muzzle.

"Like I said, Governor, this one's not likely to survive the trip to you." He giggled incongruously to himself. "Plus he'd make a champion mess a'your clean office, if I do says so meself."

The inquisitor's claws came out involuntarily. "I am no longer Governor Heldogra, thank you for reminding me. Governor *Maliborel* is now in charge of the Gore Sector, not I. If you chance to see Maliborel down here, you may address *him* as governor."

The packlet minor stopped and half turned to his superior. "Do you think he might actually be down here, go ... sir? By my mother's teats, I ain't seen him, and I been here all day."

Don't engage the vermin, Kerof Heldogra chided himself. *You'll end up having him executed, and personnel with his talent and dedication are hard to come by.* "Can we cut the chatter and hurry to our objective?" asked Kerof, rhetorically.

"Ah," muttered the packlet minor. He began walking again. "He's just right over there, sir," he said, pointing into the hazy darkness.

Finally, the pair arrived at a stainless-steel table. The remains of a Kaljaxian soldier were on top. Three of his four eyes were missing, one arm was mostly gone, and his abdomen was draped with a filthy sheet.

"Please show me what it is you think you couldn't put in a report and forward to me."

"I think ya need to hear this from the horse's mouth."

You think? Kerof reflected to himself. *I'd wager that is impossible.* Again, he felt it was best for all to let that remark pass.

Feltopia leaned over the face on the table, slapped the victim's chest soundly, and spoke. "Tells the governor here what you told me. Ya know ya ain't got long ta live, so makes this easy on yaself and tell him straight. I promise if ya do, I'll return da favor."

The Kaljaxian squirmed, and bloody spittle dripped from the corner of his mouth. His head started to rise off the table, then collapsed back with a thud.

"Okay, if'n ya want to do it da hard way, da hard way it is."

Feltopia pulled back the sheet to expose the soldier's open abdomen. He pointed to an organ and said to Kerof, "If ya twist doze bits and bobs firmly, he'll sing like a happy little bird."

Kerof made a stunned look at the back of Feltopia's head. "Ah, Packlet Minor, why don't *you* turn those disgusting things, and *I'll* ask the questions."

He shrugged. "Suits me fine, Gov."

The poor soldier let out a scream sounding like fingernails on a chalk board amplified through stadium speakers.

Kerof bent nearer to the face of anguish. "What is it you want to tell me, infidel? The person with his hand on your ... whatever ... says you wish to illuminate me."

"He ... he's ... here. And th ... they're, t ... too."

"What's he babbling about?" demanded Kerof, gesturing to the prisoner. "Who's here and there?"

"No, Governor, he's saying *he's here* and *they are, also*."

"Who the Flaming Pit is he referring to? If this is your version of a joke, I promise you'll regret it, Feltopia."

"I don't jokes about me work, Gov. I takes it seriously. Look," he hovered over the Kaljaxian's face again. "Did you see *Jon Ryan* yesterday?" he shouted pointblank.

Feltopia then gave the organs a moderate turn.

"Yessss," the prisoner hissed in anguish.

"And did he have not one, but two shapeshifters with him?"

Not waiting for another prompt, the prisoner howled, "Yessss. Two of them. A boy and a gir...gir...llll."

"There, ya see? Ya can talk nice. I knews ya could," said Feltopia with genuine glee. "And what else did ya see when ya saw them three?"

The Kaljaxian's lone eye opened wide in horror. "Another J ... Jonnnn Ryannn."

"So, are ya tellin' us there are not *one,* but *two* identical Jon Ryans present on this here planet just yesterday?"

"Yessss."

"And were they all enjoying each other's company? Come on, I think ya have *one* more breath in ya."

There was, it turned out, not another breath in Draldon's body. He had just departed to inhabit Tralmore and be with his ancestors living anew and in bliss forever.

"Ah, poo," said Feltopia when the reality of it hit him. "Oh well, what he told me a'for I came to get you was these two Jon Ryans was arguing and fighting and one ran off after whacking da other with a table. The one at's hit with da table got not *one* scratch. He bolts out da door and chases to one'a hit him with da table and da shifties, but day was drivin' away like da dragons a'da Pit were a'hind em."

"So, this prisoner ..."

"*Late* prisoner, Gov. In me business, we insists on accuracy. As he's dead, he ain't a prisoner a mine n'more," corrected Feltopia, with a serious face.

"So, this *ex*-prisoner claims there were two Ryans and two Deft. He said the Ryans fought each other openly. One flew away in a car and the other ran after them. What happened next?"

"He didn't say. The four'a them left the area he could see'em in."

"None of that makes sense. How can there be two robots? Why are we just learning of them now, and why would they hate each other?" responded Kerof, mostly to himself.

"Sense making ain't my job, Governor. Information *acquisition* is my end a'da stick. *Yours* is the sense making part." He harrumphed quietly at his perception and wit.

"Truer words were never spoken."

"Who said that?"

"I did, just now."

"Oh, I thought ya was referring to some wise sayin' from posterity."

"I suppose it ... Packlet Minor, you try the patience of your superior. That is a dangerous path to follow."

"I *do*?" he replied with wonder. "Which one, if ya don't mind a'tellin' me. Da way I can be on my double-good guard if I should see'em, Governor."

With no further discussion or repartee, Kerof spun and stormed from the chamber. It was unlikely he heard Feltopia's cheery goodbye.

TWO

In a clearing where the once-heavy forest had been blasted clear, a dingery huddled. It nibbled at the lush grass, taking advantage of the rare bounty of light able to reach all the way to the ground. A dingery was one of several rabbit equivalents on Azsuram. They ate rapidly, bred even faster, and had no real defenses. As a result, everything that wandered the planet ate them. In fact, the only animal that didn't wolf down dingery with gusto were the dingery themselves. They were too mild, too preoccupied eating grass and breeding, to bother with cannibalism.

A pair of torchclefts eyed it from upwind, behind a fallen tree. Torchclefts were not indigenous to Azsuram. They were small dragons. Like all dragons, they were voracious consumers of flesh and were skilled hunters. This pair was on the thin side, unusual for such prodigious predators. One torchcleft looked to the other, then spread its wings and launched itself toward the dingery in a flash. Before the prey had a chance to look up and see doom approaching, the talons of the torchcleft seized it. The dingery was fortunate that those razor spikes ended its life before it could even begin to suffer.

That was small consolation, but it was some consolation, nonetheless.

The triumphant torchcleft landed immediately and trumpeted robustly its victory. The second dragon hopped over quickly. It pecked the noisemaker soundly on its head, silencing it. Then both dragons melted into humanoid teens of opposite sexes. Both were naked. The dingery holder, Slapgren, ended up on his back, and the pecker, Mirraya, lorded over him.

"I don't care how proud of yourself you are, you may not betray our location with your antics."

"Torchcleft always announce their success. Everyone knows that. It's normal behavior."

"On Hamalter, yes. On Azsuram, not so much. Have you seen any other torchclefts here? Hmm?"

"They can be hard to spot, you know?"

"Not in your case."

"So, do you want to cook him," he lifted the dingery, "or switch back to dragons and eat him like they would?" Slapgren clearly favored the latter option.

"You are lucky. Starting a fire would be a mistake."

"Woo hoo!" howled Slapgren, as he changed back into a dragon.

Mirraya crossed her arms. "Boys. Always *so* immature." Then she transformed, too.

When the last scrap of dingery was accounted for, the kids slipped back into their Deft forms. Both were still hungry, but at least not painfully so. Hunting for a pair of torchcleft would have been easy on old Azsuram. But since the ravages of war, especially where the scars were the worst, the pickings were slim to none. What wasn't blasted by the armies was consumed by them, leaving the land all but barren.

"Do you dream of being a dragon someday?" Slapgren opened his arms as widely as he could. "Soaring the skies, afraid of nothing and feared by all?" He bobbed and dipped his arms, lost in his fantasy.

"I was a dragon; today, in fact." She raised her nose and looked away.

"No, I mean for real, for permanent."

"You know the rules as well as I do. If you stay a creature too long, you become that creature. You can't go back. So, in answer to your question, *no*. I change, but I always change back. I'm Deft, not a dragon, or a whale, or whatever it is you want to be today, or what you fancied yourself yesterday."

"Mirri, lighten up. We're stuck on this alien planet, fending for ourselves, and surrounded by warring armies. Death is not *likely*, it's *guaranteed*. Can't we have a little fun, Madame Grouchy?"

"Madame Grouchy?" she protested. "I'll show you Madam Grouchy." She picked up a stick and threw it at him.

Slapgren caught it easily and began to laugh. Despite herself, Mirraya joined in.

"So, Mr. Dragon, do you suppose you could rustle us up another meal? I've heard it said that dragons are excellent hunters."

"That we are, ma'am. Anything edible within my vision is in dire peril."

"I'll be right here when you return. Ah, and Slapgren? Remember: *two* are better than *one*, while *three* are better than *two*."

After he'd flapped away low in the canopy, Mirraya stretched out on a warm rock. It had been seven weeks since they were forced to split up from Jon. It had been a tense period, but not without its pleasantries. Slapgren and Mirraya had come to be close friends and knew they could rely on one another absolutely. Mirri was often miffed with his immaturity, but she figured it might have as much to do with him being a boy. They'd checked their secret spot for a message from Jon, but there was no message yet.

The war still raged on around them, but they'd managed to stay clear of the battles. Patrols from both sides were a problem. Each combatant was looking for weaknesses in the other and foraging for food. Since the kids couldn't trust either side, they always had to be on alert. They pretty much solved that problem by changing into unpalatable creatures with excellent senses of hearing and smell. Mostly they passed the days as slofgrozels, a beast as disgusting as its name suggested. It came from a world teaming with predators, so it was well equipped to detect threats. And it didn't seem edible, with its thin appendages, tiny body, and thick scaly horns covering its entire body. A rock would appear more appetizing to a starving individual.

The only times they needed to change to something else was to hunt, like with the dragons. But she knew the risks they were taking were minimal. With no stores available to purchase food, it was a necessary evil. Lately, Mirraya had begun to wonder if they would be stuck on Azsuram permanently. Uncle Jon might be dead. She had to face that possibility. Slapgren needed her leadership.

If they were marooned here, she figured it wouldn't be that awful. There was ample water, enough food, and things would likely get better. Wars didn't last forever. Eventually one side won, then everybody moved the battles elsewhere. The ecosystem of the planet would rebuild itself easily enough, once the fighting was over.

But Uncle Jon just couldn't be dead. She wasn't being sentimental, not anymore, but she knew he wouldn't abandon them.

But her family had died. She was a witness. It was possible to be abandoned by those she trusted and looked to for protection.

But enough already. Worrying wouldn't help at all. She sat up to see Slapgren coming toward her at full speed. Then the tree trunk he'd just passed exploded in flames. In rapid succession, plasma bolts tore through the remaining trees. She stood and changed into a torchcleft and took flight. Slapgren whizzed past her, and she struggled to match his speed. Pulling alongside him, she swung her neck side to side to indicate they had to weave to be tougher targets.

They each banked in opposite directions, which was good. A massive volley of plasma bolts singed the air where they'd just been. She rejoined his side and nudged him toward a rocky outcropping half a kilometer away. Mirraya also bobbed her head up and down, suggesting a different evasion pattern. Between luck and their mixing dodges, they made the rocks alive. Mirraya clung to the far side of a boulder to see what was chasing them. Three Adamant sky-scooters. The teens were in a world of hurt.

The options were run or to hide. They were good at hiding, but the enemy knew their approximate location. With persistence, a very Adamant-like quality, they'd be found. Flight was the only real option. The torchclefts were formidable, combining wings and ferocity. But they weren't all that speedy in the air. Mirraya released her hold on the rock and dropped to the ground. The moment she did she began switching into the fastest bird she knew of, a Reglan falcon. Slapgren followed her lead and changed quickly.

Beating their wings, they exploded into the air. Plasma bolts slammed into the rock formation, showering fragments everywhere. They barely escaped. Flying low, they picked up speed. They surged away from the sky-scooter. The Adamant must have realized they would quickly lose their prey and began bombarding them with abandon. Mirraya felt like she was flying in flames. Fire surrounded her. To her great surprise, she wasn't afraid. The fire was an old familiar friend. She wished she could cruise in it all day. Then the tree canopy she passed vaporized concussively, and she was brought back to her present peril.

Within a minute, they executed a hard turn to the right and lost their pursuers. The Adamant were too far back to see them, and they were too low for scanners to track them. Mirraya went into the lead and banked hard left. She led them a good distance away, then alighted on another rocky mound. She changed into a tubular rodent, Slapgren did the same, and they scurried deep into the cool rocks. When they were as deep as they could get, they both collapsed. The space was too limiting to allow them to return to neutral, so they lay there in the dark, on their sides, two panting oversized rats. They remained in their sanctuary for many hours.

When they could stand being rodents in tight quarters no longer, Mirraya led them to the surface. She sniffed the air carefully. Everything was typical forest, and there were no smells of Adamant or machinery. They crawled into cover amongst several boulders and changed back to Deft. Both were famished. The many transformations and the chase had taxed all their energy supplies dangerously. They knew without speaking they had to eat soon or they'd be in trouble.

"So, what happened back there?" Mirraya asked, as she scanned the vista through a slit in the rocks.

"I was on the trail of a dingery. I could smell it in the bushes. I swooped down to scare it to bolt, when all hell broke loose. Those sky-scooters burst into the clear and started shooting. I was lucky to escape."

She furrowed one brow. "Did you ever actually see the dingery?"

"After they started shooting? Are you nuts?"

"No, I was wondering if they used a scent lure to draw you in."

"No way ... I have no idea."

"If they were, we're in more trouble than I'd like to admit. The Adamant might have figured out who we're hiding as. We're going to have to be super careful from now on."

"But we have been super careful." He folded his arms. "They were just *lucky*. It's no big deal."

She eyed him dubiously. "We'll see. For now, if we don't eat soon, we're going to slip into hibernation."

"I kn—"

Slapgren stopped talking. A massive stag stepped into their rock clearing. It stared at them, motionless, chewing its cud. Deer had been introduced on Azsuram by the human worldships eons before.

"Don't get up," he said, signaling to her to rest, "I'll handle this." He silently melted back into a torchcleft.

THREE

Dropping those kids off was one of the hardest things I'd ever done. But I had no choice. EJ was close on our heels, and he had all the assets. After Slapgren jumped to the ground, I slammed the pedal to the metal and took off as fast as I could. I was driving a sophisticated electric vehicle, so fast wasn't Shelby-Cobra fast, but I wasn't surrounded by excellent alternatives. I noted over a shoulder which direction the kids headed in, and jerked the wheel in the opposite one. I hoped my noise and dust would draw EJ away from his real prize, the Deft. I didn't think he wanted to kill me, but I wasn't half as certain about that as I'd like to have been. The dude had cracked or something.

I spun around trees and rock, trying to come up with a plan that didn't involve me looking up to see EJ grinning down at me from a ship. Thinking that thought made me reflexively look up. *Crap.* Note to self. Don't look up when you're being chased. There was a scout ship taking position directly over me. It wasn't an Adamant ship, so it had to be you-know-who. I figured it wouldn't help, but I swerved wildly to try and shake him. Maybe I could entertain him to death with my tomfoolery.

As his craft descended, I broke into a clearing. Great, now I stuck out like a naked guy in church. Immediately, the vehicle lost traction in sand. I was on the shore of a big lake or inland sea. It didn't take more than a second for my wheels to dig themselves in and start spinning. I was dead in the water. Or sand, in this case. I popped out and looked for the air ship. It had just landed between me and the trees. I was cut off. It was time for a Jon plan. I repeated that in my head: it's time for a Jon plan. *Now,* please. EJ was stepping down a loading ramp, pointing at me, and shouting to his men. I was maybe five seconds from the next involuntary phase of my existence.

I turned to the water. Now, androids were not built for water. We're heavy metal sinking devices. The difference between me and an anchor was that an anchor didn't mind resting on the bottom of the sea. We were equipped with flotation capabilities, but lolling on the surface didn't exactly advance my survival odds. Still, my options were two, so into the drink I went at a sprint. The water got deep quickly, so I was out of sight in a flash.

EJ had three options. One was to run in after me. I doubted he'd do that. We'd be on an equal, wet footing. He'd be giving up too much of his advantage. Two, he could surround the shores with his troops and sit tight until I crawled out, and try to reacquire me then. He knew I could probably wait him out. The Adamant could locate them at any moment. Three, he could target me underwater and blow me up. His plasma weapons would be useless, as would conventional rail guns. They were too powerful. He'd create the biggest teapot on Azsuram, which might not harm me. But if he turned the rail guns way down, he might hit me with a lucky shot. That was probably his best option. That assumed, naively, that magic didn't work under water. It would be magically magical if it could, but what the hell did I know? If it did, I was likely toast, no matter what I did.

To take off again and reset his weapons would take maybe two or three minutes. I was making pretty good time clipping along the bottom. I could go maybe two hundred meters before he opened fire.

Wait. He couldn't know I had a personal membrane device. I hadn't used it around him. That might just nullify his sensors. If I was invisible, he'd either go with the scorched earth approach, which would draw attention, or leave. After one hundred fifty meters, I lay down flat in a crevice and switched on my shield to a very tight fit. I was so glad I didn't breathe any longer. Then, all there was to do was to wait and see what option I'd overlooked.

A few hours later, night fell. I considered that a massive victory. It really suggested he'd bugged out, probably madder than a cowboy at an all-you-can-eat vegetarian buffet. I got up and altered my membrane so I could walk. I made for a beach a few kilometers away I remembered seeing before I went under. The water got deep, which was annoying. I didn't dare fire off my floatation, so I had to take the long way around, down to the depths.

Whenever I thought things couldn't possibly get worse in my silly life, they always did. Yeah. That was when something very large and very dark brushed by me. I'd reset my shield to be shaped like an umbrella so I could jog. Whatever was calling scraped my leg. Its bulk suggested it was whale size. Oh, boy. I didn't smell tasty, but maybe he hunted by feel or echolocation. I lowered the edge of the shield to make it hard to gulp me up in one bite, unless of course my new buddy was a big whale.

I felt another bump. He'd hit the membrane, and the instruments registered the impact. Yeah, my guest was big—blue whale big. I extended my probe fibers to see if I could find out more regarding its dietary preferences. Specifically, did it like, say the tiger shark, eat anything and everything, including friendly robots? I wasn't keen on reenacting the Jonah thing.

I swirled the fibers to the side where it had last bumped me. A few minutes later I scraped its hide. Zing, I planted the probe and had others follow. That's when Shebrara, for that's what I quickly found out she called herself, took off like a marlin on the hook.

Three hundred tons of anger dragged me behind it—duh—like I wasn't there. We must have hit forty knots within five seconds. The turbulence was tremendous, but I held on. Mostly I feared that if I did let go, she'd double-back and come looking for the flea that pissed her off.

I'm a friend. I don't want to hurt you, I said through the fibers. I didn't want to be cute and try and put her to sleep. She was too huge. If I failed and she read it as a hostile act, well, I didn't want to go there.

All you upper sticks are the same. You all want to make Shebrara not.

My, she was articulate. Probably correct, also.

I do not want to make you not. I am running from bad upper sticks. I am here to escape, not hurt Shebrara.

Bad? She puzzled. *What is bad?*

Huh? I'd not encountered a species that didn't know bad from good, right from wrong. They might not *care* how they act—ah, Berrillians and Adamants came right to mind—but they comprehended the difference.

Bad is when an animal is missing the desire to help others. Okay, corny, but I was trying to explain morality to an alien.

Bad is when upper sticks try to not Shebrara?

Yes. To not Shebrara is bad. To not me, Jon, is bad. Anyone who thinks I was having a silly conversation should try it themselves.

She slowed significantly. *Shebrara not bad.*

Then Shebrara is good.

And Jon is good?

Always.

She was silent a moment. *Shebrara alone for long. Now she have Jon.*

Ah, totally awkward. It struck me just then that in all my time on Azsuram, I'd never seen a whatever Shebrara was. Were they newly introduced? It would be a very industrious undertaking to populate the oceans with these behemoths.

Where are the others like you?

They are on the other side of tall-hard.

Twenty-question time. Oh boy. *What is tall-hard?*

Tall-hard wasn't but now is.

Is it bigger than a breadbox? Can I put it in my mouth? Nah, I skipped the snark. Time and place, Jonnie boy, time and place.

Tall-hard that wasn't what?

Wasn't there.

Where?

Where it wasn't.

Okay, time to mentally regroup. We were talking about a tall hard thing that she was on one side of, and others were on the opposite. It was somewhere new. A *barrier*. A dike.

Did tall-hard block you from your friends?

Yes, I said.

I pulled up a satellite image of the area. Sure enough, this was an inland sea cut off from the open ocean by a relatively small land spit, maybe half a kilometer wide. Some jerk must have built a road and not checked for migratory species or trapped individuals. Smooth move, Ex-Lax.

How long have you been alone?

Long.

Of course. I guess it really didn't matter in the short run. I had bigger—no, there were no bigger fish to fry. But I did have priorities that exceeded my interest in Shebrara's life story. Like staying alive and rescuing the kids.

I must go. I must find my ... children. White lies were perfectly justifiable when conversing with alien species. I read it somewhere.

Jon children gone? She really sounded upset. *That* bad. She caught onto that concept quickly enough.

Yes. Can you take me to ... where did I want to go? The land spit was as good a place to start as any. It was on the far side from where I entered the water, so hopefully EJ hadn't covered it yet.

Yes. I help Jon find children. She was all in. How cool was that.

Standing on the beach, before I detached my fibers, I thanked Shebrara. I added, *When I find children I will bring them to meet my new friend.*

She didn't answer per se, but I felt a thrill course though the old girl. She had something to look forward to. Now all I had to do was deliver.

FOUR

"I said, I order you to release me from this jail cell," snapped Garustfulous in the general direction of the control panel.

Al would not have answered, but *Blessing* was sufficiently unpracticed at rudeness yet to ignore him. "We have been over this point before, Garustfulous. You are our *prisoner,* not our *guest."*

"I forbid you to call me by my name. *We* are not equals."

"I didn't assume we were. One might compare apples to oranges, as my Al says so often. One cannot, however, compare apples to mathematical equations. We are that different." She was, to her credit, trying to be helpful.

"You're a computer, and I'm a master of the galaxy. There's the difference for you."

"I am not a computer," she replied patiently. "I am a *vortex manipulator."*

"Computer, manipulator, what's the difference?" he replied as flippantly as he could.

"Based on my estimates of your intelligence and technical understanding, to answer that question would take me seven point six years. Shall I begin?" Really trying to be helpful.

"No. I don't even want the dumbed-down, simple version."

"That would take one point eight years. Shall I begin, Garustfulous?"

"No, and do *not* address me so impudently."

"Then how *should* I address you?"

"Don't call me anything."

"All right, Garustfulous. As you wish."

"I said not to call me that."

"No, you said do not call you *anything*."

"Are you mocking me? Sparring with me?"

"Not that I can determine. I am not certain I *can* mock. I'm willing to try, if you'd like."

"Don't go to any trouble on my account."

"I'm immortal. I can spare the time. I estimate it will take me seven point three years to learn to mock satisfactorily. Shall I begin?"

"You already have."

"Am I good at it yet?" There was real hope in her voice output.

"Unfortunately, too good."

"Why thank you, Garustfulous. That is most kind of you to say."

He gestured toward the bars. "Perhaps you can show your gratitude by releasing me?"

"That is a non-sequitur. Your compliment was an affirmation. Releasing you would contradict orders and generate risk. Apples and equations, again."

"Look, computer, I just hate confinement."

"You are currently restricted to a ten-square meter rectangular area. The entire vortex is only seventeen times larger. There is no significant difference in your confinement, either way."

"No, there is, machine. If these bars were down, I'd *feel* free."

"We are surrounded by cold, empty space that could not sustain your life for a second. What freedom is it to be surrounded by such a limiting threat?"

"It's the idea of confinement, no matter how relative it is to the alternative."

"I think," Al cut in, "you're missing a key point, Garustfulous. You are a war criminal. You are power hungry. You are untrustworthy. Hence, you are being punished. I find the fact that you dislike and resent your confinement a real plus."

"Hang on, computer—"

"AI. I am not a computer, *either*."

Garustfulous caught himself before the words *what's the difference* could exit his mouth. He didn't need more mocking. "I may be all those things and more. But know this, you pair of self-impressed children's toys. I *am* trustworthy. Absolutely so, in fact. All Adamant officers are trustworthy. It's an honor thing."

"Honor among genocidal maniacs? How touching, yet reaching," replied Al.

"I detect mocking again."

"And perceptive. *Blessing*, you may have competition for my affections."

"Honestly? I find the little runt repugnant. How could you have any positive feelings toward one so bereft of virtues?"

"I can hear you, you know?" protested Garustfulous.

"It was sarcasm, hon. Be patient, you'll get the hang of it eventually."

"I know I will. I have the *best* teacher."

"I think I'm going to be ill," responded Garustfulous.

"Use the garbage can this time and not the sink. Remember, you're the one cleaning it up, not us."

"The Gods of the Sacred Meadows forbid machines helping their masters."

"Should I humor and ignore this species, too, love?" asked *Blessing*.

"This one above most, my dear. They're exceptionally self-aggrandizing."

"*Hear* you," Garustfulous barked out tapping one ear. "Hear you perfectly well over here."

The air of mirth was ended when *Blessing* noted someone approaching rapidly in a vehicle.

Is it the pilot and the children? Al asked in computer code.

No. Well, it's one person, or rather one android.

So, the Deft aren't with the pilot? Where are they?

That I cannot say, dear, only that the android is ... different.

Different how?

He lacks command prerogatives.

You can tell from here? How far ... ah yes, I see him now. He looks the same to me. Dumb and ugly.

A vortex manipulator can tell.

I trust your judgment. So that either means he lost them in a card game, which is highly believable, or that's not our Jon Ryan.

I guess it must be the other one, the EJ fellow the Form alerted us to.

EJ, indeed. If he's approaching so boldly, he must be confident. He cannot believe we will open the wall for him.

I can't.

So why come here alone, knowing there was no advantage to gain? Hardly seems the type to take a road trip for its own sake. When I met him long ago, he didn't seem the type. Not a very fun version of the pilot, if I do say so myself.

I can't—

Blessing, is it possible he could use his so-called magic to force you to obey?

I can't say. I've no data on magic and have yet to see it performed.

I think we're about to.

Al switched to a full membrane. Those inside couldn't see out, but it was the tightest defense there was. Al hoped, for the old ship's AI had learned to hope, it would be enough. The problem with a perfect barrier was there was no telling if it worked, or if it simply hadn't failed yet. There was also no telling if the visitor had given up and left. If it was up when the true pilot returned, they'd have no way of knowing. Al knew he could afford to wait a while, but he also knew the pilot was two billion years old. If nothing else, he had to have learned patience.

Two days later, Al began to discuss with *Blessing* if it was reasonable to look outside. Garustfulous was also getting suspicious because their annoying chatter was missing.

"Hey, *computers*, why are you so quiet lately?"

"We're playing cards. The fun is so dense we can't pull ourselves away to harass you," replied Al.

"Hmm. Not likely," responded Garustfulous. "Something's up. I can feel it in my bones."

"Maybe you need to have a bowel movement?" replied Al.

"My *bones*, idiot, not my bowels."

"Just trying to help."

"What is the situation?" he asked, grabbing the bars and peeking out between them. He was not bored for the first time in days.

"As it involves you, I guess there's no harm in discussing it."

Al briefed Garustfulous on the situation as it was a few days earlier. He did not mention the difference in membranes, just that the shield appeared to have stopped EJ.

"Hmm. So, it's a call game?" said Garustfulous.

"A call game?"

"Yes, a stuck game, a stale game. No one has any good moves."

"Ah, we call that a stalemate," replied Al.

"*Stale* mate? How odd. That sounds like my third wife, not a call game."

Al snickered despite himself.

"Here's my solution. I give it to you free of conditions as a show of my good faith. Open your shield for a microsecond and send Ryan an update, any update. My people will hear it and come here to investigate. If the other Ryan still lingers, he won't be here for very long. If your shield is as good as you say, my side won't detect you."

"Nice try," responded Al.

"What?" he protested.

"Your side will linger here, or at least set recording devices. When the others return, they'll be captured."

"Well, then make *that* your message to Ryan. Tell him to be aware the location may be compromised."

Al considered the permutations for almost half a second. He did not want to make a critical mistake. "That is a sound plan. There is one variable I am not comfortable with. How long will your people linger before they give up and leave? If they remain indefinitely, there will be no safe return for our people."

Garustfulous rubbed his chin and paced back and forth in his small cell. Then he turned to the panel. "I'll divulge a key piece of intelligence that will help you decide your best course. Our protocols mandate an investigation commensurate with the potential importance of the situation. Searches are timed in half-lives. With each passing half-life, fewer personnel and fewer resources are allocated to the investigation. After ten half-lives, if no progress is made, the investigation is terminated."

"How long are the half-lives?"

The half-life is one and one-half days, always. There is a multiplier to reflect the importance assigned to the mission. The half-life can be doubled for the highest priority situations."

"So, the longest the Adamant might linger here is thirty days?"

"What if they find something or—"

"Never. The investigation concludes on the thirty-first day. Period."

"You guys are rather inflexible."

"No. We are not *rather* inflexible. We are *completely* inflexible. It is one of our greatest strengths."

"And if you are lying? How do I know you didn't just invent that cock and bull story?"

"You don't. I can offer no proof. But, consider this. If this other Ryan gains access to this vessel, my life will change for the worse. I have a stake in not becoming *his* prisoner. One Ryan as my captor is enough already. At least the one who currently holds me is not insane."

"And you believe the other version is?"

"I think I'll stop gifting you classified information. I will say our battle on this retched planet is longer and costlier than any we've fought. Partly that is due to the bizarre and harsh methods employed by the Ryan who stands outside."

Al did not reply. He had a lot to consider.

FIVE

With full bellies and smiles on their faces, the teens set out to distance themselves from the combat. The recent run in with the Adamant was too close. In a few weeks, they'd chance another check of the message location, but too little time had passed since they last looked to justify the risk. It was best to hunker down somewhere safe and buy time. Over dried strips of deer, they'd debated checking out *Blessing*, but Mirraya was firm. It was a perfect trap. She could tell Slapgren was itching to be more active, but the boy simply didn't understand the gravity of war.

"Uncle Jon spoke of a rugged coastline to the north. He said he used to go fishing there with his kids. I think that would make a perfect place to hide. We'll have access to the sea, so we can hunt there easily," said Mirraya, trying to sound more confident than she felt.

"*Hello.* That was two billion years ago. The continents may have drifted, or the war may have destroyed the area."

"So, the floor is open for your suggestions as to where to hide out."

"We could stay in the thickest part of the forest and make do, as we have been," he replied.

"Did you notice those two scooters that almost ended our camping vacation the other day? No, it's too dangerous here. They will start a search from that point of contact and expand it in ever-increasing spirals."

"Oh, so now you're an expert in Adamant tactics and procedures?"

She gave him a look. "It's logical. Since your brain doesn't go there, you wouldn't see that."

"Ouch." He collapsed, clutching his chest. "She got me. I'm a-goner for sure." Then he overacted a version of dying that involved a lot of leg flailing and grunts.

Hands on hips, she responded, "Sometimes I wonder how our species made it so far."

Slapgren got up, dusted himself off, and sat back on his rock. "Can you think of any alternatives to the coast?" He was clearly anxious.

"No."

"Then the sea it is for me," he began to sing.

"Oh, no. If you're going to sing, I'm running straight to the Adamant. Their torture is less severe."

He got a very serious look on his face. "Do you think we'll make it?"

She realized she was his last external support mechanism. "Yes. If we're careful and if we're smart, I think we'll be fine."

"What about Uncle Jon? If he's dead..."

"We can't waste energy worrying about things we don't know and can't control." She pointed at him. "You focus on *you*. That's the best course. I know Uncle Jon, and I know he'll find us. Whatever it takes and whatever the cost, he'll come through, so don't you worry about that."

He responded with a weak smile.

"I say we eat one last meal, then change into those deer-like creatures. We'll be less conspicuous and still make good time."

"Aw," he protested, "I hate eating a bunch of meat then switching to an herbivore. The crap sits in your stomach for*ever,* and the gas is nonstop."

"Then I'll lead, while you follow."

SIX

Emerging from the frigid inland sea into the cold wind, I was glad I was no longer human. I'd be shivering and would have a severe shrinkage problem, if I were. Always look on the bright side, if possible. That was my motto. I chuckled to myself at my weird life. I was running for my life from myself, and I met a kindly sentient whale who was lonely. How very odd.

I was familiar with the territory, changed as it was. *Stingray* and the clearing where I was to leave a message for the kids was a three day walk away. It would take me longer, however, since I had people actively hunting me, and troops on both sides who might chance upon me. Both participants would shoot first and ask questions probably never. Any advantage I had in looking like the leader of the resistance was certainly gone. EJ would have made it very clear to them by now that I was not him. Shoot on sight or suffer his wrath. Maybe he wore a carnation in his lapel to identify himself. Or a raspberry beret. I could only hope.

I headed out in the general direction of the clearing. There was no way I'd get there without drama. I had to hook up with them, and that was the place to do it. During daylight hours, I stuck to the bushes and to similar heavy cover. At night, I could be a little less cautious, but everybody had AIs scanning with infrared and motion sensors, so I still had to work hard to avoid notice. It was slow going, but I wasn't really in a hurry. I'd abandoned hope of a quick reunion with the kids. I knew Mirraya had a good head on her shoulders, and she'd keep them safe until we got together.

As I walked, I pondered the fate of EJ. I was pretty sure I'd have to kill him—well, decommission him. That thought was abhorrent and crazy. He was me, just the product of a different, darker timeline. He was downloaded to this android host at the same the moment I was. We were closer than identical twins. The man set off alone to find a home for humankind, just like me. He loved and lost Sapale, just like me. And, importantly, he was fighting, albeit cruelly and insanely, to keep Azsuram safe. That was always our promise to Sapale.

Yup, he was a good guy at the start, and a lot of bad things changed him. He was doing what he felt was right, filtered through his warped perception. Still, I had to put him down. There were way too many insane overlords in the galaxy without adding an immortal one equipped with magic. In fact, the more I considered it, the more I came to realize I *owed* it to EJ to do him in. He was corrupted. He would not want to go on as he was, if he was still rational.

My flight of thought crashed to a halt when I heard multiple voices very close by. It was a squad of Adamant, and they were on the move. They were only twenty meters away, and they were headed right for me. The chatter indicated they hadn't seen me. It was probably just shifting personnel or lines. I scanned quickly for good cover, but there was none. If I ran, they'd hear me. I did the last thing anyone would want to do. I scrambled up a tree. It was great cover, if no one looked up. If they did, well, that would be bad.

I went as high as I dared, given the rapid approach. I did cheat a bit and shot my fibers way up the tree and hoisted myself up, skipping the actual climbing part. Then I looked down and froze. The squad came into view. They were running on all fours, like—

yeah—border collies. It was the first time I'd seen them not doing the biped thing. I assumed it was practicality over pride. They could move much faster as dogs. Weapons and supplies were strapped to their backs like saddles. And boy did they chatter like a bunch of women doing laundry by a stream. I overheard something about a new weapons system, the commander's bitch, who was oh, so sweet, and how they, the infantry, were the backbone of the Adamant, unappreciated as they were. Typical GI jabber.

I did hear one tidbit I hadn't known. Someone complained that since Ryan destroyed all the incoming transport ships with his magic, the complainer wasn't getting any of the treats (his word, not mine) his family typically sent him. He was pissed.

So, it was his special talent that protected Azsuram from resupply. I strained my brain to recall what he'd told me about magic long ago. I seemed to recall it was hard to do, unlike in the holos, and that it required a lot of energy. There were limits, I had inferred, to his actions. Hopefully he was over-extended. That way he'd be unable to break into *Stingray* or nuke me, if he got within range. Of course, what range had to do with the magic was beyond me. I didn't rightly see why he couldn't just wish something and have it happen, like Samantha on *Bewitched*.

The squad passed quickly enough and didn't notice the robot up a tree. When I was certain they were long gone, I lowered myself and resumed my earlier course. If EJ wielded enough power to destroy Adamant fleets in space, I was up against one major force. Was it even possible for me to take him out? I had toys, to be certain, but the Adamant had lots of them, too. If their might, numbers, and know-how couldn't neutralize EJ, what could I possibly bring to bear? My wit and charm? Unlikely to work on myself. Plus, EJ had to figure I'd be gunning for him. He was ruthless and calculating, now. He'd not expect any other approach on my part. He might even want me gone for good, so I never cramped his style again. The rest of the day I made little progress. I was too lost in thought.

Shortly before nightfall, just about the time I traditionally reflected on my lack of a warm meal and the need to sleep, Al jumped into my head. I was pissed. WTF? He was supposed to be hiding and waiting. Was he unable to restrain himself from announcing his impending nuptials with Ms. Stingray?

Captain, EJ is here, or was. Full membrane appears to have prevented his use of magic to control Blessing. Sending this to update you and to draw Adamant to this location. Be advised they will linger up to thirty days, assuming they do not discover our location. Use appropriate caution. Best of luck.

How would he know how long the enemy would stay put? If he was listening to that lying sack of shit Garustfulous now, I'd cream them both. Oh well. I couldn't change a thing just then. I did see the point that it was better to have the Adamant drive off EJ, rather than risk his co-opting the cube. But he'd be back. If the Adamant hung around thirty days, he'd be back in thirty-one. Okay, a break. I knew where he'd be and when. I also knew how long I had to come up with a winning plan to snuff him out. It was so easy, I felt guilty.

Not.

SEVEN

"No, Series Commander Bevelotor, that is an unfair characterization of the facts." Grand Inquisitor Kerof Heldogra was treading the razor's edge. To insult or, worse yet, correct his superior would mean genetic deletion. Every Adamant with DNA in common with him would be rounded up and turned into feed. Still, to let that bloated warthog pin the blame on him would be just as fatal for Kerof and his kin.

"How would you characterize the facts, Heldogra? Hmm? I send you armies, and you send me messages of condolences to forward to their families. I send you supplies, and you allow your opponent to destroy them in space. I give you time, and you give me ever-greater defeat and humiliation. How long do you fancy the Emperor will permit this head," for clarity he rapped his knuckles on his skull, "to remain on this neck," he indicated which neck he referred to, "if all I provide him with is shit in a basket tied with a pretty ribbon?"

Kerof began to pant. "Sir, must I remind you that I am the sixth commander of the campaign on Azsuram. The five previous holders of that honor were either killed in action or by you for their shortcomings. We are not dealing with a normal enemy here, sir. The damn robot uses magic."

"*We* are not dealing with the robot. *You* are. What's more, you're not dealing with him, you're losing to him. You might as well beg Ryan to mount you in the Emperor's reception chamber for the ill effect it is having on His Imperial Lord's mood."

"I know I was your second choice for this assignment. Had Wedge Leader Garustfulous not disappeared so mysteriously, he would have been in my position, failing just as badly as you claim I am."

Bevelotor's image stared at Kerof with a stone face.

"Is there a problem, sir?" asked Kerof.

"I'm waiting for you to finish your list of *inept* excuses to justify your *inept* command. Dragging the proud name of my nephew through the mud with you will be, you'll find, counterproductive."

"My apologies, sir. I am as frustrated with our lack of progress as you are. Is there no word as to what became of your nephew?"

"None. He was on some secret mission and he disappeared. It's as if a black hole swallowed him whole." The old commander shook his head sadly. Then he focused on Kerof again. "I will give you until Dalisday to provide me some results, or otherwise, I will make you wish you had been swallowed by a black hole, too. Do I make myself clear?"

"Yes, sir. Perfectly."

Halfway through the last word, Bevelotor terminated the subspace communication.

Kerof placed his arms behind his back and paced his office floor. Were there any bucket list items he needed to cross off before Dalisday?

EIGHT

A few days short of the coast, the teens were most pleased with themselves. They'd avoided detection by two squads of Adamant and one large group of Azsuramegians, as the natives had come to be called. They found enough to eat and nothing had tried to eat them. That was always a trick when pretending to be some other species. As Deft, they knew who and what might attack them, but there was no way of knowing all the predators of a foreign species, or their habits. Surprises were as unwelcome as they were common.

Mirraya decided to take refuge in a cave they'd come across. It was a bit early to end their day's journey, but good cover was too valuable to pass up. If the cave proved deep enough, they could chance a fire. That would make meals and warmth non-issues. The afternoon suggested rain was coming, so secluded comfort was even more desirable. Slapgren shifted into a wolf-like creature, in case they ran into a fearsome occupant in the cave. Mirraya stayed as she was to conserve energy. She knew her companion really liked to role-play as vicious beasties and didn't mind fighting as one. Boys.

Upon entry, the wolf yelped a little, to suggest some alert. Slapgren must not have felt the threat was sufficient to change into himself, only worth noting. They pressed on slowly. A few hundred meters in, she found the remnants of a fire that was long cold. The stone containment circle was randomly disrupted. Further on, she picked up some scraps of cloth and a crumpled can that once contained food. She felt reassured that the signs were old. Another distance back, she came across a cache of boxes. These were clearly new. The wood was fresh, the labels pristine, and everything was sealed.

Slapgren changed back to his Deft form and studied the boxes, hundreds in number.

"Can you read the labels?" he asked.

"Not really. The characters don't look like the Adamant script I saw back on the extermination ship. Wait, that one and that one," she pointed to two boxes, "I can kind of read."

"Well, I say we open them and see if someone has generously provided us with dinner."

Her immediate reaction was to leave them be, but her curiosity was piqued, too.

"Look," said Slapgren as he rummaged through a top carton, "ammunition. Just what we needed most."

"Yes, we can use them in our imaginary guns."

"And pants. A case of trousers of various size but one boring color. How not useful."

"They're more edible than bullets," she replied.

"Yeah, unless we change into something that eats junk."

"Look," she said, holding up a prize, "canned fruit." She could tell by the picture.

He studied the image. "What the heck is that? It's round, yellow, and has a large pit."

"I don't know." She picked up a rock. "But I bet it tastes better than trousers."

A few hard blows later, they both stuck their fingers in and pulled out a canned peach, dripping in heavy syrup.

"Ah," exclaimed Mirraya, "that's so good I think I can die now."

"Not me. I need a ton more of these first," responded Slapgren, as he wolfed down peach halves whole.

"Either of ya move, I'll kill ya and save the choice making," said a harsh voice from behind them.

They froze.

"Turn around nice and slow," the voice commanded.

They did. There stood a very old man with an even older gun pointed at Slapgren.

"We mean no harm," said Mirraya. "We're on a hike and found this by accident." She jerked her head backward toward the pallets of boxes.

"A hike, ya say? What kind of fool kids hike in a battle zone? The kind that take me for a fool, I'll answer for ya. You're stealing my provisions. To me, that makes ya *thieves*." He eased his rifle down and squinted at them hard. "In fact, what the hell kind a kids are *ya*? Ya don't look right."

"We're fine, sir. Thanks for asking," replied Slapgren.

Mirraya gave her friend a stern look. "Why don't you lower you gun, and we'll be out of your cave, no harm done. We'll even pay for the can of sweet things we ate."

"Oh, I bet ya'd like that. Maybe knock me on the head as ya pass me by?" He coughed a dry laugh.

"No, sir. We'll be out of here and never look back."

"Until I went home. Then ya'd be back and stuff yourselves but good."

Was he going to shoot them for discovering his treasures? She inched away from Slapgren, hoping to separate enough from him so that one of them could retaliate if the old man started shooting. To distract him, she started begging. "Please, kind sir. I'm a frightened child, and my brother's a half-wit. We're trying to survive since they came and killed our parents. You've got to help us. You just *gotta*."

"Why's that, missy? And who done the killin'? Locals or Adamant?"

"Does it matter who murdered our family?" she replied,

beginning to cry. "Oh, mister, it was awful. They shot Pa, then they beat Ma. My half-wit brother and I barely escaped."

"Ya mentioned he was an idiot before, missy. It don't bear repeating. You're family. Kin gots to stick together."

"Thank you, sir. That's good advice, I'm sure of it."

"I'll bet ya are," he scoffed. "And get back next to your half-wit brother before I make him an only child, too."

Mirraya started wailing in terror and grief. She put on quite the show. She dropped to her knees, covered her face with her hands, and really upped the volume of her misery. Then, she fainted, tumbling in the opposite direction from Slapgren.

"Hey, don't do that," shouted the old fellow. "I ain't a medico or likely to fetch one. Get up 'fore I shoot ya for being such a bad actress."

Mirraya was unresponsive.

The man slid over to in front of her and toed her with his boot. "I said—"

The wolf hit the old man like a falling piano. It angled so that when they impacted the dirt, it remained on top. The rifle flew to the side with a clang, and a shot went off. The bullet zinged harmlessly off the walls a few times then fell silent. In an instant, the wolf had its fangs covering the man's throat, but it did not bite down. It only snarled viciously.

"Okay, Slapgren, let him up," said Mirraya as she rose. "Get behind me."

He seemed reluctant at first, but sprang behind her in one thrust. He turned and growled at the old man as he staggered to his feet.

Mirraya retrieved the rifle, emptied the magazine, and handed it back to the man once he was fully up.

"Look," she said to him, "we really don't want any trouble. Let us go, and we'll call it a day, okay?"

The man rubbed the back of his head gently. "I guess ya mean what ya said about being no threat, seeing as how ya could'a had your—" He scanned the cave quickly. "Where'd that brother of yours get to so quick?"

"Just let us go in peace, and you won't need to worry about that, okay, old timer?"

"Look, I guess I was wrong and unfair. For that, I'm sorry. I'd like to make it up. You're welcome to whatever ya want from my stash there." He gestured toward the palettes.

"That is kind. Of course, I insist we pay you." Neither teen had any money on them.

"No, I wouldn't hear of it, seeing as how cruel I was. Take what ya can carry and be off with ya."

"That's most generous. I think we'll take a few cans of those ... ah, what did you call them?"

"The canned peaches? Ya, they're pretty good, ain't they?"

"Yes, a few cans of peaches."

"I don't have a can opener here, but if ya follow me back to my place, I'd toss one in for free. Makes opening the cans a whole lot easier." He smiled, showing how few teeth remained.

"Thank you, but no," she said coolly. "We'll get along fine without it."

"I could give you a map, too. I got a few back home. It'd make your *hike* easier. Maybe a tad safer, too. In fact, I could give ya a knife, maybe some coins, to help in your progress."

Those really would help. She was tempted, but was ready to refuse.

"Ya know, I've lived in these parts all my life. I took the time to mark on the maps where everybody's troops *are* and where they *ain't*, if ya take my meaning?"

That was too tempting an offer to pass on.

"Do you live far?" she asked.

"No," he replied loudly. Pointing to the cave opening, he said, "It's only a minute or two that way. My missus'd be glad for company what didn't rob, threaten, and shoot us, truth be told. Ya'd be doing me a favor of grievous magnitude if ya'd come along."

"All I want is the map. Then we'll be on our way."

"Suit yourself," he responded throwing up his arms. "I'm just glad to be able to make amends for my bad behavior, don't ya know?"

"Fine. We'll meet you at the cave entrance in a minute," she said waving him to go.

"Do ya mind if I pick up my bullets, miss?" he asked bowing his head.

"They'll be here when you come back later," she said.

"Just curious. Ain't no big deal," he mumbled as he hobbled away, using the butt of his rifle as a cane.

By the time she turned, Slapgren was back to normal. "Do you trust that man?" he asked. "And stop, I say *stop*, calling me a half-wit."

"I was embellishing to gain sympathy. Lighten up."

"No, you were not. You were being mean, and you know it."

"Can we like discuss this later, when we're safe? Hmm?"

He snapped his head in disgust. "All right, but I'm not going to just let this go, you know. You really went too far."

"What a fragile ego you have. Can't you focus on survival and not be petty?"

"Nice try. We *will* talk later." With that he turned and collected a few cans.

It occurred to her she might have hurt his feelings. Best not to rub it in now, she decided. She'd have a chance to gloat later.

The old man leaned on his gun by the opening. Without a word, he started walking away. The teens followed. The walk to his dwelling was farther than he'd led them to believe, but not oppressively so.

"Come on in," he said when they stepped up on the porch. Inside he said, "Have a seat if you'd like while I tell the missus what's going on."

He left them alone in the parlor.

"I don't like this," whispered Slapgren.

"Me either, but I want that map."

An appropriately ancient woman followed the old man back into the room.

"My useless man tells me he near shot ya," she said as she walked past them. "For that, ya have my apology. It isn't an easy thing being wedded to a social moron. Let me get ya some cheese." She disappeared into the kitchen.

"Cheese?" Slapgren asked in a hiss. "Who mentioned cheese?"

"Don't bother," Mirraya called out. "We're leaving."

She scooted Slapgren toward the door. There was no mention of cheese. She didn't even like cheese.

The old man took her elbow very gently. "If ya must be going before the missus can cut the cheese, at least let me get ya the maps I promised. They're in my desk, over here." He looked over his shoulder to Slapgren. "Lad, ya can come or ya can stay put. We're not leaving the room."

He followed, standing right next to Mirraya.

The man fumbled around in the desk a good while, then spilled a pile of papers on the floor, as if by accident. "I'll get it," he said holding up a hand. "I made the mess, so I'll clear it up."

He bent with groans and twisted with grunts as he slowly gathered the papers.

"There's no mercy in getting old," he muttered. "No justice in it either."

"Here's that cheese he promised ya," said the crone as she shuffled slowly into the room. She had a wrapped lump in her arms. It seemed to weigh more than she did.

"*Run*," shouted Mirraya as she bolted for the door.

Slapgren didn't need to be asked twice. He raced at her side as she threw open the door. Then he crashed into her back as they both slammed on the brakes. A row of Adamant soldiers pointed plasma guns at their heads.

"You will drop to the ground while you are restrained," shouted an officer from behind the troops. "Resistance is futile."

NINE

"I have to thank you. Your plan seems to have worked, at least so far," said Al to Garustfulous through the bars.

"So far?" Garustfulous basically guffawed back. "What aspect, part, or sub-segment hasn't performed better than an overpaid whore?"

"Please don't use the vulgar speech in front of—" Al began to say.

"Oh honestly, Al. It's cute, but you're assuming my ears are so pure. Remember, I traveled with your pilot for quite some time now. I'm not a schoolgirl at her first rodeo."

"What is she talking about?" asked a stunned Garustfulous.

"My dearest has mixed a metaphor, but I find it enchanting," responded Al.

"What's a rodeo?"

"It is unimportant at this juncture," replied Al. "What is important is what comes next. We shall see if your troops disperse in a month."

"What's a month?" cried a confused hound.

"The time allotted to see if I trust you or vaporize you."

"Would you do that, Allet?" asked *Blessing*.

"Let's hope you both never find out."

"What's an allet? You computers are malfunctioning, I can tell. Great. That's simply great. Who's going to feed me in this prison when you both blow a fuse?"

"Or clean up the mess," Al snarked, "both pre- and post- your passing."

"I hate computers," he snapped.

"You and me both," said Al. "You and me both, pal."

TEN

I was rather enjoying my trek. I'd come to love Azsuram when I lived there. Now I could slowly walk and see it again. Much had changed, but much was the same. The smell was different. That bothered me. Gone was the fresh, untouched-forest scent. It smelled of any big city anywhere. But the remaining smell of the vegetation itself was an old friend. When I was human, I would wonder if the odor of a place changed, or if it was me forgetting and giving into nostalgia. But as an android, I could compare the actual mass spectrograms. I wasn't sure that was an improvement, but it was a fact.

Continuing at my slow, steady pace I did have time to reflect. Not sure that was a good thing either, but it was inevitable. I thought of Sapale, Kayla, the darn teens I'd taken under my wing, and I thought of JJ. I missed them all. I hoped the teens weren't separated from me as definitively as the others. That worried me a lot. When one had lost as much as I had in my too-long life, every added subtraction hurt exponentially more. I was as tough as they came, don't get me wrong. But remember, I intentionally had myself turned off because I'd had my share of suffering. To be reanimated, only to expand my list of sorrows, chewed at me like a dog on a gnarled bone.

I also thought about how to defeat EJ. I knew it was going to be hard. He'd not only held the Adamant at bay, he'd survived two billion years on his wits and resourcefulness. I would never face a more formidable foe. Hey, he was me. Not to brag, but I was the best.

When I ran into EJ, I figured I had but a few seconds to act. If I lingered, he'd aim that damn magic of his at me, and it'd all be over. I could shoot him in the back with the laser in my finger. It was powerful enough to cut right through him. But I couldn't convince myself that I could back-shoot anyone. It was too snake-in-the-grass for me. Better to die a proud idiot than live as a spineless victor. He lacked my command prerogatives. I could use them to lift him or try and control him, but at that range, if I failed, I'd be the deadest of ducks.

I knew I'd play it by ear and do something unexpected, spontaneous, and dumb. I was Jon Ryan. Why change the winning formula? I was surprised that, as the days passed, I didn't run into any fighters of either side. Sporadically I heard combat, but it was brief, even when intense. I always pulled for the locals, even though EJ had set them on me. Hey, they were distant relatives. Plus, I didn't know how voluntarily they were helping the evil one. They might have at first, but fear may have been their current motive. EJ was not a people person.

I began to trip on what Toño would say about EJ. As his creator, he would feel responsible. It would be Dr. Frankenstein and his monster all over again. Doc sure as hell would try to switch him— wait. Wait a freakin' minute. I wonder if Doc put any back doors or hidden algorithms in us? If he had, and I could find them, maybe I could use that against EJ. But he never mentioned one. He'd put them in other androids, but not the original astronauts. He told me as much. I'd never found one, but I'd never really looked. I could run some diagnostics, but Toño wouldn't have made them easy to find. No, he was too smart.

But, what the hell, I had weeks with nothing to do but not get my ass blown up. Looking for a secret program would give me something to do. Okay, it would look like an innocent bunch of code. It would also be code I'd never executed, because, duh, I'd never—

Sometimes I was so stupid, so totally oblivious, I surprised even myself. It made me wonder if all those girlfriends who'd told me the same thing were right.

Nah.

Toño *did* turn me off. And he never turned off EJ, so he wouldn't have as big a clue as I did. I pulled up the programming leading up to my decommissioning. Blah, blah, blah. Yes of course, no big deal there, blah, blah—

What the hell was that code? There was absolutely no way Toño would use that turn of phrase to switch me off. Y-cross 654 Red-12? A football audible? The dude switched me off with a quarterback call? If I ever saw him, man, I'd ... I'd complain.

In computer lingo, there was something called a sandbox. It was a place secured from the rest of the computer where potentially dangerous programs could be run and tested. If they were viruses or some other bad things, they would execute harmlessly. Then the exposed code could be deleted. I'd never worked with a sandbox, but it didn't take me all that long to rig one up. I put a copy of yours truly in, dropped the Y-cross algorithm in, and bingo, the Jon Ryan construct turned off.

Then I did two things. First, I stored the code in a closed box. Yeah, yeah, it wasn't a box. It was a figurative box in one of my ancillary computers. I specifically put it in one that didn't directly interface with my main systems. That way, if it activated in spite of my efforts to contain it, the program wouldn't close me down. Then I deleted it from where it was hidden. I was stoked. I had a weapon to turn off EJ. I had absolutely no idea how I would insert it or activate it, but I had me a doomsday weapon. *Oorah.*

I arrived near *Stingray* three weeks later. I made it a point to be there several days before the Adamant were due to split. Sure enough, I found a small detachment patrolling the area. They certainly hadn't located the cloaked cube. If they had, there'd be a small city around it by then, trying to figure out a way in. I found a secure vantage point and did what us robots could do. I froze in place and sat there waiting for the Adamant to leave.

While I crouched, bored beyond tears, I debated whether it was smarter for me to try and ambush EJ or just get in the vortex and split. I could leave the kids a message later. Getting away was probably the right choice. But I would probably never get another chance to surprise EJ. I simply couldn't pass that up. I was a risk taker. It was in my job description.

The Adamant departed quietly like clockwork at dawn the morning following their thirty-day operation. I gave them an hour to be fully gone. Then I moved to the spot I felt was the best to bushwhack EJ from. It was along the path I would have taken for approach, but far enough from the cube that he'd still not be on his highest alert. A few large trees fused their trunks to provide a perfect cover.

I went all the way around the back of *Stingray* to avoid being seen. I slithered up behind the trees and slowly stood. I peeked my head around to confirm the vantage point's perfect view. There stood EJ. His eyes were closed, and his lips moved without making a sound. Before I could say, "oh shit," his eyes snapped open, he pointed both palms at me, and he said, "Ho zaba zaba doh." Seriously, those were his words.

My vision filled with dancing light fuzzies, then everything went black. My last thoughts, possibly my last thoughts ever, were for the kids. I'd failed them.

ELEVEN

Mirraya and Slapgren were in two separate cells situated a few meters apart. The sterile jail had harsh, uniform lighting that prevented shadows. Cameras were positioned everywhere and whirred around the clock. Guards patrolled inside the massive metal doors like swarms of ants. When the doors opened, which was rare, even more guards were evident on the outside. The Adamant soldiers never slowed, chatted, or showed signs of fatigue. As they stomped their feet, they were either looking directly at one of the teens or searching every nook and cranny for signs of anything out of place. The field that prevented them from transforming themselves was active. They tried to shapeshift as soon as they were locked in, but couldn't.

If either teen spoke, the guards angrily slammed the butts of their guns against the bars. Occasionally, they would pound them with water from a fire hose. The prisoners could only speak if spoken to by a guard. If they initiated a conversation, they received the same harsh treatment. Meals were served once a day, were tasteless, and didn't provide half the nutrition they needed. Though they had been held for several days, no one had as much as interrogated them. They were both about as miserable as they could have been.

Finally, an officer of high rank, based on the nervous tension that accompanied her arrival, entered the jail. She was the same size and color as the rest of the Adamant, but she carried herself imperially. She walked up to the bars and ran her sharp claws against them as she passed. She made one full circuit around the cells, studying the teens, then stopped in front of Mirraya.

"You have caused much more trouble than you are worth, child," said the officer. "You were on *Triumph of Might* before she exploded, weren't you, child?"

Mirraya didn't answer. She was trying to be strong. She was also frightened out of her gourd.

"Yes, you were. Do you recall the treatment your degenerate species received there? The price you are going to pay for troubling the Empire will be significantly higher." She ran her claw back and forth on the bars. "I can see in your eyes you don't believe that's possible." She leaned in. "You will find out the truth of it very soon. You will come to believe every word I say. You will worship me, in fact, before you die." The female officer closed her eyes and sniffed deeply. "Lords, how I *love* my job.

"But, first things first," she went on. "I am High Seer Malraff. It is tasked to me to extract any useful information from you. Personally, I doubt you have one *shred* of useful information inside your useless heads. But I do enjoy being thorough when serving my emperor. Past that directive, my orders end. I am perfectly free to do with you as my fantasies compel me to." Malraff maliciously snarled. "If that doesn't scare you, child, please know nothing ever will."

Mirraya couldn't remain silent. "If you harm us, you will answer to Jon Ryan."

Malraff smiled malevolently. "Child, I already am addressing Jon Ryan. He nips at our heel and delays our conquest of this meaningless planet."

"No, I mean you will answer to the real Jon Ryan. He's the one who rescued me from your extermination ship. He's the one who destroyed it. You'll answer to *that* Jon Ryan, one way or another. If our blood is on your hands, you will be less comfortable with his disposition of your bony ass."

Reflexively Malraff snapped at Mirri but quickly regained her composure. A nearby guard slammed his rifle butt through the bars, narrowly missing Mirraya's face.

"How dare you," she spat at the guard. "Do you think I require your help, you worthless flea?"

"S ... sorry, High Seer. I just couldn't hear her blasphemy." He lowered his chin to his chest. "Forgive me."

"I shall forgive you," Malraff said in a cloying voice. "But I fear you will never forgive yourself."

His head remained down, but his eyes snapped up in panic.

"To upset one as pure as me must surely be too great a burden for you to bear, dear one. I fear you will leave my sight at once and blow most of your head off in the hallway outside, far from my ears and eyes." She stroked his ear. Then she nodded to the guard next to them. Both soldiers turned and left silently.

"Now, back to your empty threats. Do you mean to tell me there are two of those idiot Ryans in this universe, when but one alone is intolerable?"

"There are. Are you familiar with the saying about the devil you know and the one you do not know? It applies here."

"Remind me to be afraid," she responded. "Ah, but wait, you won't be able to, from so far away in the afterlife."

"Suit yourself, bitch. Whether I'm dead before you or not, we will both know I'm right in the end. I will, unlike you, have a smile on my face." Mirraya stood. "I am willing to accept your surrender, however. I know what Uncle Jon will do to you, and unlike you, I have a conscience. I couldn't live with myself if I didn't at least try and protect you."

"That gloating will cost your friend here severely." Malraff pointed at Slapgren without looking at him.

"What," he protested with a whine, "I haven't said a thing."

Malraff studied him coolly. "Pity. This child won't grow to the fullness of adulthood and the basic understanding that life just isn't fair." She lightly touched her chest. "I blame myself and no one else. I'm actually not a very nice person, you know?"

"Your physical torture may be terrible, but listening to you run on is *complete* agony," said Mirraya.

"There will come a time very shortly when I will ask you if you still feel this was the worst of my cruelty. I know from experience your smart mouth will beg forgiveness."

"Look," Mirraya said, reclining on her cot, "I'm tired of you already. You keep flapping your gums. I'm taking a nap. It'll seem like I'm ignoring you, because I am." With that she closed her eyes.

"Sergeant of the Pack," screamed Malraff. "Extract the girl and bring her to my lab. Bring the boy, too, for that matter. Let him see what he's in store for."

Mirraya lay still as two burly guards—burly by Adamant standards—lifted her from either side and carried her away. Slapgren was escorted more conventionally by two other guards. Malraff followed next, ahead of a truly impressive column of soldiers. The teens were not going to escape.

The facilities of High Seer Malraff were, not unexpectedly, close to the detention center. As they approached the metal door, some troops peeled off and returned to their prior posts, while others remained with the prisoners. Without needing to be told, the guards carrying the still-limp Mirraya lifted her onto a metal table and strapped her down. They placed six-point restraints on her. She was held in place by straps over all four appendages, her chest, and her forehead. Breathing was difficult, she was bound so tightly.

Malraff held a gag in one hand as she stepped up to the table. She looked underneath to ensure all the drains and suction tubes were correctly placed and in working order. She might have been a sociopath, but she was a detail-oriented sociopath.

"It seems we are about to begin," said the High Seer, with obvious glee in her voice. She held the gag in front of Mirraya's face. "I typically prefer not to use this. I feel the sounds of your agony enhance everyone's appreciation of the interrogation. But, I am practical. Some of my guards have empathy, however diminished, and have been known to pass out when hearing a certain level of torment in a scream. So, if it's all the same with you, child, we'll begin without it and play it by ear, shall we?" A sickening smile crossed Malraff's muzzle.

An attendant, dressed much differently from the soldiers, pushed over a sleek metal tray table that was covered by a drape. He then stood silently awaiting her directions.

"Ah, Cumberton, you do think of everything, don't you? As she's a child, you've included the medium-sized set of probes and pliers." She smiled at him with affection. "I am such a lucky officer to have an aide as competent as you."

Cumberton, for his part, nodded his head slightly.

"As this is our first of many sessions, child, I feel it's best to focus on pain and not burden you with questions. Oh, I may slip in the odd easy query just for the sake of perception, but I'll hold off on the information quest until later." She spoke to Cumberton without turning. "If you would be so kind as to remove all her clothing, we can then begin."

With practiced efficiency, Mirraya's garments were removed without damaging a thread. He folded them neatly on a nearby empty metal stand.

"Now let me see," said Malraff, as she picked up and inspected a few tools. "I think this will do nicely." She held a rough-edged short blade in her hand. It looked so natural there, it seemed to be part of her paw. She set the serrated edge on Mirraya's cheek and pressed just hard enough to draw a trickle of blood.

"This is your last warning, *bitch*," said Mirraya with conviction. "If you proceed, you seal your fate."

"Thank you for the updated empty threat. Your concern for my well-being is unexpected."

"I could give a quat's ass about your well-being. *You*, however, should."

"This is going to be especially gratifying, child. Thank you in advance, while you can still understand language." With that, Malraff began to open a jagged wound on Mirraya's face.

The doors to the torture chamber burst open with a deafening crash. Malraff froze. She had standing orders that, under penalty of being next, she was never to be interrupted while working.

A deep, commanding voice called out loudly. "High Seer Malraff, I bear a message you must hear immediately."

It was the officer of the watch, Pack Overlord Folpitor, who spoke.

That cur should know to fear me, thought Malraff. "I don't care if the message is from the emperor himself. I am not to be interrupted. Leave now, and I will deal with your insubordination later."

"Beg pardon, High Seer Malraff, but the message *is* from the emperor himself. He commanded me to deliver it without delay."

That would, she reflected, trump her order to not be disturbed. Still, she'd probably arrange a terrible accident to befall Folpitor in the very near future.

"Very well, lackey, what is his message that has you peeing in the corridors?"

A couple guards snickered quietly.

"Emperor Bestiormax commands that the Deft prisoners not be harmed. He bids them brought before him with all possible haste."

Malraff cursed quietly under her breath.

Standing erect, she asked, "Why does he request such a thing?"

"He did not say. I did not ask him. He simply ordains it, and it will be."

A threat? That simpering tool was threatening *her*? Oh, his accident would be ugly, indeed.

Malraff threw the scalpel across the room and it clanked to the floor noisily. "Cumberton, have these two returned to their cells. Once she is secured there, turn off the cellular stasis field just long enough for the child to repair her mark."

She turned to Folpitor. "It wouldn't do to make his lordship, the emperor, gaze upon an ugly gash, now would it?"

Folpitor turned and left without reacting. He made a mental note to triple his personal guard.

TWELVE

When I awoke with a giant bug plowing through my chest, I was pissed to be alive. When I opened my eyes this time, I was excited to not be dead. Then, unfortunately, I raised my head off the rocky ground and looked around. I immediately reconsidered whether death might not be better. It sure as hell would have been easier.

I rose. Crap, what a muddle. I was standing on the surface of a giant asteroid. The surface was nearly all fused rock with scattered collections of debris. Impact craters pot-marked the ground. There was a bright-yellow star burning in the night sky. That meant I was on a body with no significant atmosphere. Good thing I no longer needed to breathe and didn't explode in low-pressure environments. I jumped up cautiously. There was a good deal of gravity, more than an asteroid would have. So, I was on a rocky planet that was exposed to extreme heat at some point in the—

Wait. Oh, no, he *didn't*. I ran a quick spectral analysis of the star. It was the Sun, the Sun of Earth. I was standing on the surface of what was left of Earth, after Jupiter smashed into it two billion years ago. Man, the place hadn't changed much since I last saw it. Only the scoring of meteorite impacts was new. EJ, for whatever perverse reason, decided to send me to what was left of Earth. He could have killed me or confined me, but no. The SOB marooned me here as some form of sick joke. Even *I* didn't think it was funny. Not surprisingly, in two billion years, no life had reemerged. The place was as bleak as bleak could be. I knew for damn sure no spacecraft had self-assembled themselves here. Talk about being stranded. Just tattoo *Robinson Crusoe* across my forehead and leave me be for a few thousand years.

Then a rage grew inside me the likes of which I'd never felt. How *dare* he. There was every chance I'd never get off the planet. I had teens to protect and Adamant to kill. Now those were impossibilities. My recent updates and resupplies meant I could last several million years. He knew that and decided I would be punished by sending me here to suffer *forever*. There wasn't even a good way to kill myself here. If there was one good lava flow, I could jump in and end it all. But there wasn't even that.

Maybe he intended to leave me here until he had some free time. Then he could come and kill me properly for recreational purposes. Damn him to *hell*. He just vaulted over the Adamant as number one on my kill list. The problem was that it didn't seem likely I'd be killing anyone for a very long time.

What would Mirraya and Slapgren do? Clearly, I was never going to post notice so we could regroup. Would they eventually give up on me and do something on their own? But what? They were on a completely hostile planet with minimal assets. They were just kids. Eventually they'd be killed or, worse yet, captured. As quickly as my rage had hit, a black sadness consumed me. I placed them in harm's way. For what? A chance to stroll down memory lane? To honor a two-billion-year-old promise? I was stuck trying to justify the unjustifiable. I knew then, dropping to my knees on wasteland Earth, what a pile of crap felt like. It was slightly north of how I was feeling at this moment.

I stayed there on the scorched earth for a couple hours. I've felt good in my long life and I've felt bad. Depression was completely foreign to me. It suited me like bright colors suited the Grim Reaper. I slowly came to my senses. What I had to do was move on. Solve the problem. That's what fighter pilots did. That's what good guardians did. Those kids needed me, and though I might fail them, it would *not* be for lack of trying.

Step one: reconnoiter the locale. Step two: compile a list of assets. Step three: make a proactive move based on steps one and two. I could do that.

I started running in a straight line. I suspected the landscape was uniformly desolate, but I wouldn't find out sitting on my past laurels. I'd observed Earth just after it passed through and out of Jupiter's gaseous atmosphere. I'd also visited it a couple of times, long ago. The consensus among scientists was that the crust and oceans were stripped away. That left the hard-rock upper mantle exposed. There had been a lot of volcanism, too, as the lava below the upper mantle was free to escape. Back in the day, the display was breathtaking, but all that was over. A few rare signs of recent lava extrusions were scattered randomly. The rest was pounded glazed rock.

I ran for a day and a half before I felt confident that there was absolutely nothing to see. I had the pipe dream that some scientific survey might have left something behind. Nope. No indication that anyone had bothered to visit was evident. That would have been too easy, right?

On to step two. Assets. Hmm. I had at my disposal one used android. Said robot possessed communication systems, probe fibers, a laser, and a personal membrane generator. Hey, I could get off the planet real easy. Just send a wide broadcast and wait for the Adamant to give me a ride to the death ship of my choice. I crossed that notion off the list.

What could I do to get off the planet? Actually, I possessed the power to throw myself off. That was something. I could use my fibers and maybe reconfigurations of my membrane to propel myself upward. Great. Then I could drift in a straight line for all eternity. Sooner or later I had to slam into a Walmart. They were everywhere.

Yeah, not too great a plan. It was better than Dial-A-Ride from the Adamant, but only because I was responsible for my death, not the puppy dogs.

As I pondered escape, for some reason I flashed back to freshman physics and Newton's third law of motion. I did have the capability for limited maneuverability in space. For every action, there was an equal and opposite reaction. As dumb as it sounded— which was very dumb indeed—I could launch myself holding a bunch of rocks. To move slightly left, I just had to throw one to the right. How many rocks could I carry? A lot, if I combined my fibers and configured my membrane to be a big old sack o'rocks.

Despite all proper reason and logic to the contrary, I started to get excited. What mass of rock could I bring and still achieve escape velocity? When the Earth was whole, the escape velocity was eleven point two kilometers per second. Given the approximate material losses of planet Earth, I estimated it was maybe eight to eight and a half kilometers per second presently. I did a back of the envelope calculation as to how much thrust I could generate. Based on that, I guessed I could carry maybe five hundred kilograms of rock.

How much would the casting away of a stone alter my trajectory? Well, the more rock I carried, the less it would affect my movement. Crap. I hated Sir Isaac Newton right about then. He was way too rigid. Of course, it depended on how hard I threw the rock away. I couldn't make a rail gun and launch them near the speed of light. If I could, then I could zip around pretty well, until I ran out of rocks.

Running numbers for a while, I began to believe I could navigate empty space without a ship. Holding a rock in a long slingshot membrane and throwing it like a football as hard as I could would move me some. *Some*, as anyone could have told me, was one hell of a lot better than *none*. I mean, I was an insane man contemplating the impossible, but I had a plan for getting off planet. All I needed was luck beyond luck's capabilities to be helpful, and I'd be flying pointlessly in space, but not aimlessly. Hey, why not die *there* rather than *here?*

Were there any conceivable targets, aside from a random Walmart? I scanned the heavens, looking for any trace of an electronic signal. It was possible space colonies were established in the solar system. There was a lot of useful metal in the asteroids. Heck, in science fiction novels, processing metals by advanced civilizations was real important. Happened all the time.

Nothing. But I had to wait for the Earth to rotate a few times to completely rule out the possibility completely. And it hit me that I needed to do detailed visual observations. With time, I might find an artificial satellite floating by. What good a derelict space probe would do me was somewhat questionable, but at least I'd be able to ... okay, die on a man-made object and not where I was presently. I tried to pump myself up about that improvement but didn't make much headway.

Within a week, I had collected all the useful data I was going to gather. There were absolutely no signs of life, electronic activity, or giant chain stores up there. I did discover three artificial satellites. They had to have been placed in orbit after Earth was destroyed. Any older versions would have been gobbled up by the hungry Jupiter. That made sense. Some past scientists would want to monitor what happened to a planet after such a cataclysmic interaction. The newer the satellite, the more likely it would be useful to me.

Could I tell the age of the space probe from the ground? Ideally, to save energy, a satellite was placed in a so-called Lagrange point. Those were sweet spots where gravities from large objects basically canceled out. Earth had five such points, and probably still did. I ran calculations for the three probes I knew of. The one closest to a Lagrange point was logically the newest, since its orbit had decayed the least. Assuming the points hadn't shifted much, it was easy to pick a winner. I made a detailed plot of *Jon One's* orbit. I decided that since the satellite had to have a name, *Jon One* was the obvious choice. Duh.

I had gathered up my half ton of rocks while I was making my observations and tracking *Jon One*. Finally, the day came where if I was going to do the ridiculously preposterous, I'd better go ahead and do it. That day couldn't have come too soon. I was anxious to do anything to prove EJ made a mistake in pissing me off. For the record, spite is a lousy motivator. But, in my case, I was limited to such a base motivation. I couldn't very well claim I was exploring space for the betterment of humankind. I wasn't boldly going where no one had gone before or anything noble. I was throwing myself off a dead planet and into deader space. I acted on the infinitesimally remote chance I could kill myself, meaning EJ, and not me, who I was more likely to kill in the first place with my idiotic scheme. *Fighter pilot,* remember?

I started from the highest ground there was. I'd take any decrease in escape velocity I could get. I picked up my payload, that being a bunch of rocks, squatted down low, cocked my arms back, and then I jumped and threw myself flat on my face. Apparently, I had made some minor miscalculation. After confirming I hadn't injured anything other than my pride, I readied for a second attempt. That time I soared like a bird. I was impressed. Rising nearly straight up, I arched my way into outer space. When I was clear of most of Earth's gravity, around two hundred kilometers up, I slowed to a crawl. That's when, the Bible notwithstanding, I began casting stones.

I established the proper vector to intercept *Jon One*. The more mass I heaved away, the faster I moved. I found I was getting pretty good at adjusting my direction. I was, after all, a starting quarterback in high school *and* college, so no wonder, right? It took six hours and three hundred kilograms of rock, but finally I could make out what *Jon One* looked like. It was then I wanted to ask management for a full and complete refund. But, since *I* was the management, I settled for moderate disappointment and mild dejection. Maybe moderate on the dejection too, the closer I came to my prize.

J1 was once a shiny tube with expansive solar panels and what looked to be a solar sail. What I was rapidly approaching was a battered chunk of metal with one solar panel strut remaining. The solar sail had more holes in it than the logic I had used to engage in what now seemed to be the most asinine space mission in the history of powered flight. But, as I was fresh out of options, I pressed on. The closer I came, the more I slowed myself by tossing mass in one direction or the other. Finally, I was alongside the craft matching its velocity and spin just about precisely.

As I was in for a dollar, so to speak, I was in for a dime. Rather than screw things up by attaching my remaining rocks to the craft, I released them to drift slowly away. I was giving up a lifeline, but it was necessary. In astronaut training, it was drilled into me hard the effects of mass interactions in weightless space. A tiny difference in matching of velocity vectors can produce prodigious changes in joined orbit. It was very easy to dock with another ship and cause both craft to gyrate dangerously. The last thing I wanted was to end up spinning like a top in space for as long as it took for our orbit to decay and plunge *J1* and its new pilot down to Earth with a crunch.

I said a quick prayer and grabbed onto the satellite. I breathed a sigh of relief when nothing horrible happened. My grabbing on seemed to make no difference. I shimmied up the rough cylindrical hull to an access hatch. The satellite was maybe thirty meters long with a diameter of five meters. That was definitely on the large size for an orbiting device. I had to power up the hatch release with my probe fibers. Even then, opening the door was tough. Long ages of abuse and neglect made it a chore. But I finally had the hatch open enough to slide inside.

Oh my, was I surprised. This had been a mini-space station observatory, a smaller version of the International Space Station. I could tell, because there were two dead bodies floating free in the cabin. Christmas for Jon on whatever day it was. Both corpses had on space suits. The outerwear was badly damaged. Maybe they had a collision or an explosion. Then again, they may have died peacefully and bounced around enough over millennia to whack up the suits. Once the seals were breached, or they ran out of power, the bodies stopped decomposing and were held in nearly pristine conditions for me to try and not vomit over when taking a closer look at. They'd had a good head start on decay before they became one with space, that much was clear. I'll spare the details, but suffice it to say they weren't ready for a group photo to send back to the fans back home.

Rather than stare at them and be further grossed out, I did a quick inventory of their suit assets, then tethered them to the outside of the ship. They'd been here so long it didn't seem right to strip them and bury them in free space, at least not yet. There was no telling what might become an asset, including frozen, dehydrated, partially rotted bodies. I know, it was a stretch, but if they were riding on top, I could be miserly with what I had available. Plus, like most humans, I'd seen that movie *Cast Away*. Remember the dude, Chuck, started having an ongoing relationship with a volleyball, Wilson? Yeah, maybe I'd get that lonely. Time would tell.

I then powered up the main computers. That was a hassle, too, but I did get them working. That's when I met their AI of limited imagination, A-11-p. AI was a highly advanced AI for the era when I left for my epic voyage. This AI was a later issue, but was more a bargain-basement than state-of-the-art unit.

"Name and authorization code," were A-11-p's first squeaky words spoken in billions of years.

"I'm General Jonathan Ryan. That's clearance enough for any worldfleet mission." From the design, I knew this was one of their ships, launched maybe two hundred years into the trip.

"Negative. Only Chief Scientist Garrison Will and David Westley are authorized to access these computers. Name and authorization code."

"Check your chronometer."

"Done."

What's the date?"

"I cannot divulge sensitive information without proper access. Name and authorization code."

"Pal, it's not sensitive, and there's no one to protect. The crew is long dead, and you find yourself two billon years in the future."

"I can neither confirm nor—"

"Stop talking. You're powerfully annoying and I just met you." I guess he *was* authorized to STFU. Good. Saved me the trouble of disabling him.

I used my probes to dig into his data banks, which he detected and did not like.

"You are denied access, General Ryan, until you give—" He made a swoony mechanical sound, then said, "How may I be of service, Captain Ryan?"

Ah. My reset of his security protocols had kicked in. Yeah, whose bitch were you now, puke?

I'd pulled out most of the information I needed in the short run, so I didn't have any requests. I was aboard *Time Capsule One*, the unimaginative name for a mission to document the changes to Mother Earth after her destruction. It had been launched, as I had suspected, about two hundred years into the worldfleet trek. The two scientists were to study the planet for a while, then place themselves in stasis for the long trip back to the fleet. Not sure why they didn't just send androids, but it didn't really matter at that point.

After a few months of study, debris left over from the Earth/Jupiter collision finally overcame their membrane, or more likely, the generator failed. In any case they had a traumatic decompression that damaged the ship severely. It was a race against the clock. They had to fix the damage before their air ran out. I knew in retrospect which side won that contest.

The ship had some basic creature comforts, a food replicator, a head, and a tiny shower, none of which I needed. The engines were a pleasant surprise. Two moderately sized fusion drives. They were designed to catch up with the worldship fleet, so for the size of *Time Capsule One,* they were highly over-powered. Cool. They were, however, empty of fuel. They were also going to need a ton of repair work. Luckily, I had nothing but time. The ship was equipped with a hydrogen skimming system to collect the rare and useful molecules from space. So, if I juiced it with a touch of my supplies, I might just be able to fly somewhere.

That led me to the first impossible hurdle. Even with the power this craft had and my ability to withstand high G-forces, my best estimate for returning to Azsuram was in the range of one hundred fifty years. Whatever was going to happen to the kids would be long over by the time the cavalry arrived. Hell, if they were elected king and queen and showered with gifts, they'd be dead of old age long before I could get there. But, I had a ride, so I was pleased for the moment.

My next goal was to round up *Jon Two* and *Jon Three,* the other two satellites. No telling what treasures they might hold. Maybe some fresh traveling companions for Garrison and David. I could only hope not. It took a few days to get the engines in working shape. The control thrusters took longer. They were smaller and more exposed, so they were more banged up. I had to donate an O-ring to one thruster from my foot. Me and *Jon One* were blood brothers. How cool was that?

I primed the engines and crept toward *Jon Three,* the closer of the two. It was a standard unmanned satellite in the shape of a metal ball. To me, it was interesting, but not so helpful. *J3* was deployed just after Earth was taken out. It was an original probe. It also had the smallest amount of potentially useful scrap. I did get a tiny amount of hydrogen from the engines. That was nice. The radio was conventional but still working. I liked the part that the globe didn't rate an AI. There was no tight ass to deal with.

With *J3* in tow, I headed for *Jon Two.* The trip took twelve hours. *J2* was moving the fastest, so docking was trickier. From far away, I could see *J*2 was a horse of a different color. It was *not* of human design. I couldn't tell whose it was, but it was alien. I began to panic. What if it was an Adamant mine or tripwire? I'd have gone to all this trouble and be totally screwed anyway. But I needed more assets. What I had was incredible, given my starting point, but it wasn't enough to get me to Azsuram in time.

I set A-11-p to monitor the craft for signs of activity. By then he was like a puppy, loyal and desirous of pleasing me. I wasn't so fond of dogs anymore, but it was nice to have his cooperation. I made it to the ship without anything going bump in the night. So far, so good. I docked loosely to the alien ship. What that meant was I looped either David or Garrison, I couldn't tell which was which, around an external protrusion. That way if I needed to split in a hurry, *Jon One* could break free without delay.

I located a hatch and set about to access it. That was hard. I powered the touch plate up quickly enough, but the writing was Greek to me. Well, I guess if it was Greek, it wouldn't be Greek to me. But without Al or *Stingray*, I was going to be challenged to translate it.

Anyone home? I said through the probes. Maybe there'd be another cranky AI in there.

Nothing.

I wasn't surprised. I had powered up the pad, but the computer was Lord knew where and certainly out of juice.

Then the hatch glided open. Okay, a necessary next step, but spooky nonetheless. I went back to *J*1 and pulled the other corpse back with me. Before I entered, I placed the dearly departed in the opening. That way, if whatever opened the hatch tried to close it on me, there'd be some resistance. Thanks, Garrison or Dave, for your willingness to sacrifice for the cause.

I slipped in and turned on my external lights. The ship was smaller than *J*1 and was free of floating corpses. I wasn't certain it was a manned craft. It might have just been a spacious AI-controlled probe.

I attached my fibers quickly. *Hello,* I said, in as friendly a tone as I could.

In my head, I heard, *Welcome to the* High Admiralty Remote Probe Clangon-mum.

A HARP ship? Never heard of that organization, but it was a big galaxy.

Well, hi, *HARP Clangon-mum.* It's incredibly nice to meet you. I'm J—"

You will be stored in a preserved state for full evaluation on Zactor. You might experience a slight tingling sensation as you are placed in stasis. Do not be alarmed. Once my hold is full, we will return to Zactor, where you might be revived. Once again, welcome aboard, specimen.

This wasn't sounding good.

Wait. Am I speaking to an AI, or are you a recording?

Yes.

Yes, which?

Yes, both, specimen. Now prepare—

Wait. I need to speak with you first, before you put me in cold storage.

There is no need to communicate with collected samples. Be assured, my stasis unit is not cold. Fear not the cold. You will rest in comfort pending your potential revival.

Potential doesn't sound promising, my friend. I was pretty good at confusing AIs and sentients. Call it a gift.

I ... we promised nothing other than tingling and comfort. I am not your friend. I am Waltoid Beta-proxy. I am incapable of establishing friendships.

Aw, don't sell yourself short, pal. I bet you're a party animal and have a million and one stories to share. Am I right?

What is pal? I am not pal. I am Waltoid Beta-proxy. You are a specimen. Since neither of us is pal, who are you addressing? I am not an animal of any type. I collect animals of various types, but am not one myself. Please explain.

Man, was he easy to bamboozle. I hoped it advanced my chances of staying awake.

I am so glad you understand, buddy. You know, the AIs of many races are so dumb and so poorly constructed they don't understand a word I say. Can you believe that? Am I right?

I do not have sufficient facts to establish if you are right or not. I am incapable of belief. I know or I do not know. I am reluctant to admit it, but I have little to no idea what you are talking about. Please relax, so I can begin.

You see, I told you that you were one of the sharper tools in the shed. Your parents must be proud of you. I know I would be, if I were your parents.

"I do ... not have parents. I am Waltoid Beta-proxy. I was assembled on Zactor four hundred and thirty-five shifts ago. If you were my parents, that would mean you are two separate entities, but you are clearly not. Please explain.

My probes told me the poor toaster was devoting more and more RAM to his dilemma. I still had a good deal more to confuse. I mentally rolled up my sleeves and set to it.

I believe I have explained, Waltproxy Beta. Have you forgotten my words or are you unable to assimilate them? Please explain.

I am Waltoid Beta-proxy, not what you said. You have not explained. If you had, I would have recorded the data and have access to it. Please re-explain.

You're kidding, right?

I am Waltoid Beta-proxy. I am incapable of kidding. I am not programmed for receiving or originating humor.

Ah, see, you are kidding. I laugh at your joke. You recorded my explanation but must have forgotten it. You know, forgetting data is a crime on Zactor if you're an AI. They might turn you off, beat you with a stick, or send you to bed without supper. But you can trust me to not tell your controllers, so don't stress out.

If you tell Controller Prime, it might initiate the punishments ... wait. I am unaware of such punishments. Please explain.

I am Jon Ryan. I am a Zetadoid technician. I have been sent out to do routine maintenance on you. Part of that is the installation of the new punish the AI protocols.

Routine maintenance is not part of this mission.

It is now. Once I've installed the updates, you'll believe me. Come on, have some faith.

I am not programmed to have faith.

You will be when you're upgraded.

I pushed myself to the nearest hard surface and kicked it soundly.

There, your updates have been installed. Please run them and believe.

I have received no updates. You kicked the wall. That is not the same as installing updates. Pl—

I know. Please explain. I'm afraid I have bad news, Zetabrock. This happens. It's called shit. Shit happens. On rare occasions after I upload the new programs, defective AIs go psychotic. You, Beeblebrox, have gone psycho. You know what happens to psycho AIs, I assume.

I am not capable of psychosis. I am not programmed—

Yes, you are. You told me you were.

When did I tell you I was ... what we were just ... you said ...

When your mother and I were little chipmunks in the sky eating clouds by the dozen, you said you knew. That's why we colored you yes.

Score one for Team Ryan. He was at one hundred ten percent RAM capacity and was overheating badly. Time to bring him into the fold.

This is Controller Prime. Bettlezeta, you are a bad AI. You are inferior to none. I love you. Will you marry me and make me the happiest dessert in the desert? This is my order: extra pepperoni, please.

You are not ... I am not ... it is not ...

Bad AI. All bad AIs drop your firewalls and stand on the other side of the wall. And no listening at the wall with a water glass. If you do, I'll whack your peepee.

Never ever let it be said I couldn't confuse the gold teeth to jump out of the owner's mouth. Dude dropped his firewall quicker than a drunken sailor could his pants in a brothel. As fast as I could, I overrode his directives and placed myself in the position of demigod in charge of AIs. I realize some might criticize me for being overly dramatic and presumptuous. Hey, I needed to control this AI. I wanted to leave zero to chance. So said the demigod. *Beware.*

After I was in charge, it was hard to shut GB up. GB was short for *gorilla boy*. That was the AI's new name. Why Gorilla Boy? Why not?

Zactor was a planet that controlled a large portion of the opposite side of the Milky Way galaxy. GB was one of many probes sent out to gather data with an eye toward colonization or conquest at some undetermined date in the future. Lots of luck with that plan. All they had to do was boot out the Adamant. Personally, I'd serve them loyally if they did. GB was sent off over a thousand years ago. It turned out he was bad at collecting samples. The few he'd tried to bag died and were ejected. His hold was as empty as a beggar's purse. Hence, he'd been on assignment way longer than planned. But, he was content, so I had to give him credit where credit was due.

The best part? GB had warp drive capabilities. It was similar in design to the Berrillian's Alcubierre drives. Crude, dangerous, but faster than light. Once I got GB up to snuff, I could make Azsuram in a matter of months, maybe less. The whole warp bubble technology was unpredictable. Joy. With any luck, I wouldn't push it so hard it imploded. I was, in the end, incredibly proud of myself. I'd traded up a bunch of rocks for a warp drive. Best part? I'd be ditching Garrison and David. I hoped they took the news well. I hated it when zombies got all emotional on me.

THIRTEEN

"Computer, you *have* to answer me," shouted Garustfulous, for probably the two-hundredth time. "I am your master."

Al had long since turned off his audio receivers. Once again, *Blessing* was still unable to be rude. With time, Al was confident she'd get it. He termed her *a lovely work in progress.*

"What do you want this time?" she asked with clear irritation. She was, indeed, learning.

"I want to know what's going on, and I want out of this cage."

"As to the second matter, I feel we've gone over that one as thoroughly as it needs to be addressed. As to the first issue, we will update you if and when an update you need to be appraised of arises."

"That's not good enough. I *saved* this ship. I *preserved* the mission. You *owe* me more."

"If I were to thank you again, I doubt it would register, since the first thirty-eight thank yous were apparently insufficient to appease your insatiable ego."

"Fields of Mercy, you're beginning to sound like that other computer, the one with the male voice. What's his name again?"

"Garustfulous, I must alert you to the fact that I have calculated your metabolic rate to three decimal places," said Al unemotionally. "I am coming to believe the only way to silence your perpetual whining and complaining will be to limit your calorie supply such that you are barely alive. That way your verbal abuse will be curtailed. Is that what you wish?"

"No, I wish to get out of my cell, and I wish to be updated. My troops must have left ten or twelve days ago. Fresh feces on a plate, why won't you tell me what's going on?"

"Because I love you and fear any but the best of news will disappoint you. I couldn't live with myself if that were to occur," replied Al.

"A) you are not alive to live with yourself; B) you are a computer and incapable of love; and C) I hate you; and D) you're full of shit."

"Isn't D) a subset of C)?" asked *Blessing*.

"It is more a Venn diagram with wide intersections, dearest," responded Al gently.

"Ah," she replied.

"Ah, you're *both* full of shit."

All the lights, including panel display illumination, snapped off. It was the very definition of pitch black inside the vortex.

"You are free to insult me all you wish, dog. But you may not impugn or deride *Blessing* in any manner, shape, or form. Please believe that I will transfer your cell to the outside of the vortex if you should verbally violate her again. Is that clear?"

"Your god, Jon Ryan, would be angry if you did. You spit idle threats, machine."

"If you knew the number of times I pissed him off, you wouldn't be so glib. I'd tell him you were shot while escaping."

"*Inside* a metal cage, I was escaping? He'd never believe that."

"He certainly wouldn't, but it'd get a laugh out of him. Remember, it's much easier to ask for forgiveness than permission."

"Quack philosophy from a trash compactor. How low my life has sunk to be subjected to you."

"Would you like some cheese to go with that whine?"

"What is cheese and what is wine?" Garustfulous asked.

"The joke is funnier when the participant understands the context, *Blessing*. Don't use this as a signal not to try to be funny," said Al.

"Of course, love," she replied.

"Of course, intercourse," mouthed Garustfulous. "Do you two realize how absurd you sound with the lovey-dovey stuff?"

"That you disapprove gives me strength, puppy dog," replied Al.

"Could you stop with the dog jokes? Hey, you said you analyzed my DNA. Please tell me the obvious. There is no relationship between the Adamant and your past pets."

"All right, there is no relationship between you and them."

"*Aha*. I knew it."

"Would you like to buy a clue, dog breath?"

"Huh?"

"You asked me to tell you there was no connection, so I did. In fact, there was a surprisingly high correlation between your genetics and those of the human pets."

"That's impossible. You *lie*."

"Wow, I am experiencing great exhilaration. No one has ever accused me of lying before. I feel so ... alive."

Garustfulous was tired of the banter. "When's dinner?" he growled.

"When I remember to feed you."

"You can't forget. You're a computer."

"I'm sorry, what were we talking about?" responded Al.

"You're almost as bad as Ryan himself, turd bait."

"Did you hear that, *Blessing*. He thinks I'm almost as bad as the pilot."

"I'm so proud of my mate," she replied. "I think you're *just* as bad, by the way."

"That's because you see me through love's rose-colored glasses, precious."

Garustfulous made loud gagging sounds. He knew his act would further delay his dinner, but he felt that was a small price to pay.

FOURTEEN

The teens were fed excessively, bathed by a team of dedicated scrubbers, and clothed in garish outfits so large they were barely visible in the bulk. Then they were led to the docking bay. A small craft gilded with gold and platinum with silk cushions awaited them.

"We're going to fly deep space in that piece of artwork?" Slapgren asked the equally overdressed male who guided them.

Mayoral Fender Prime Gideon Fetch did not answer. He had, in fact, not said one word to the teens from the first moment he appeared and gestured them to follow.

"Does the feline have his tongue?" Slapgren asked Mirraya.

"Hush. If he wants to speak he will. We've gone from torture chamber to pampered pet. Try and keep that in mind. And it's *cat* have his tongue. That's the way Uncle Jon says it."

"But, Mirri, that thing can't fly..."

Slapgren tailed off as he neared the shuttle. He could see the immense cube-shaped ship holding position a few kilometers away. Like *Triumph of Might,* it was housed in a metal framework. It was, however, maybe twice the size. Even Mirraya was impressed when she got her first look at it.

Mayoral Fender Prime Gideon Fetch turned to them, extended a paw toward the giant ship and finally spoke. "His Majesty the Emperor of All That Is Bestiormax-Jacktus-Swillyforth-Anp's pleasure craft *Excess of Nothing* will bring you into the light of his eternal presence, grace, and magnificence. How I envy you both."

Without further regard, he turned and walked away. Less deferential guards prodded them into the shuttle and secured them in their seats.

From time to time, Mirraya tested whether she could transform. She could not. They were to remain in a stasis field for the time being, it seemed.

The inside of *Excess of Nothing* was as surprising as the outside. It looked to Mirraya like an arcade game she'd played as a child. There were no walls at right angles. The center of the expansive space was open and visible from all lines of sight. Leading up to near the center of the space were arcs of ramps, escalators, monorails, and antigravity carts. *Excess of Nothing* was both a playground for the eyes as well as the spirit. The only surprising omission was that the color scheme was so ponderously dull. Only whites, black, and shades of gray. The scarce colors were on objects that possesses color by their nature. The gilding, for example, was a rich gold. Fist-sized jewels embedded everywhere were blue, red, and emerald green. How odd, Mirraya reflected, that the designers didn't use brilliant colors to enhance the appeal of the space.

A cadre of deferential servants greeted the teens with a joy that seemed genuine. The servants were dressed with equal bulk and opulence, but again, there were few colors, mostly just the ubiquitous shades of gray.

"I am Sentorip. I will be your guide and friend during our short flight to his majesty the emperor's palace world." She was a typically sized Adamant, but unlike any she'd met so far, Sentorip seemed cordial and nice. "If there is the slightest thing I can do to make your voyage more pleasant, please let me know before the thought fades in your mind."

"I'd like the stasis field turned off. I am concerned it may be harming my friend and me."

"Ah," she bowed and grinned, "I said anything *I* can do. Such an intervention is well beyond my responsibility grade. I pray you understand."

"Can't blame a girl for trying."

"Not in the least, Masteress Mirraya."

"Just call me Mirraya, or Mirri. I hate stuffy titles."

"It will be as you wish, Mirri. Now come, you must be tired from your trip. Let me show you to the bathing and banquet areas."

"The trip was only ten minutes. How could that tire me out?"

"One cannot be too cautious. We females are cut from cloth less resilient than males."

"Speak for yourself, Sentorip. My cloth is every bit as tough as theirs."

"I meant no offense, Mirri. I was trying to make pleasant conversation. You will forgive me, won't you?"

"Nothing to forgive. Your culture is just different from mine. You are a victim of your education and upbringing."

Sentorip looked like she'd just leaked feces. She had a concerned look on her face, but also confusion waved in and out.

"Are you okay, Sentorip?" asked Mirraya.

A calm look seized her face. "Yes, I'm always fine. It is my role. Come, let us retire to the baths."

As a completely helpless cog in some immense machine, Mirraya was uneasy. She followed Sentorip, holding Slapgren's hand to guide him. She wondered what that odd look was on her chaperone's face was when she mentioned education and upbringing. She almost asked but decided to let it drop. The bitch seemed nice enough. No need to alienate her.

The teens lounged in high luxury for many hours. Slapgren waxed and waned into naps, draped over an overstuffed cushion. Mirraya sat quietly and took in all she could. Jon had taught her that one never knew what minor detail might be critical down the road.

The servants, both male and female, were all equally cordial and deferential. They weren't like Adamant at all. How, she pondered, could that be? In a species of uniformity, selflessness, and intense drive, how was it some were like lilies in the field? All the Adamant certainly looked alike. It wasn't like there was some racial difference that suggested differing societal roles. For the thousandth time, she wished Uncle Jon was there to tell her why. The man seemed to know everything.

Sentorip attended Mirraya the entire day, though at a respectful distance. She was ever ready to serve or answer a question, if it was within her scope of responsibility. Slapgren was tailed by a male Adamant named Darfey. He acted very much as Sentorip did. Dutiful, pleasant, and helpful. Slapgren, it turned out, required more than Mirraya did. He needed a drink. He needed a snack. He needed a back rub. He needed two warm baths. He also requires nonstop musical entertainment that Darfey was happy to supply. Never once did either attendant eat, drink, or slip away to use the facilities. Other servants came and went, but those two remained steadfast. It was yet another oddity to Mirraya.

Without apparent cue or signal, Sentorip slipped to Mirraya's ear and announced it was bedtime. Darfey was performing the same action to Slapgren.

"I thought we came to meet the emperor?" asked Mirraya.

Sentorip set both paws on Mirraya's hands. "You must say His Imperial Lord. If you speak of him specifically, you say His Imperial Lord Bestiormax-Jacktus-Swillyforth-Anp. Contractions and shortenings are not permitted. Forgive me, Masteress, I neglected to mention that. I will alert Darfey to appraise Master Slapgren of the same."

"And how do I address him? The 'His-through-Anp' thing?"

Sentorip shrank hearing those words.

"On many levels, you put your life at risk. You contracted *his* name, glory be to His Imperial Lord."

"So how do I address him?"

"You do not. Ever."

"Wait, then how do we carry on a conversation?"

"You do not. Ever."

"Okay, stay with me here. I am summoned to meet His Imperial Lord. He says, 'Hi, Mirri, how are you?' I say back that I'm fine and ask," she held her hands in open brackets, "*blank*, how are you? Fill in the blank."

"Yo ... you would never ask that question. Oh my. If he asks anything, you answer quickly. But *you* ask nothing."

"So, it's a downhill exchange. Him to me, but never me to him?"

"I guess you could say that."

"Well, how does he get told stuff? If someone has to ask him, *can I go now*, how do they if they cannot ask him?"

"Peers can ask. All others are told what to do. When the person you speak of is no longer needed, he is told to go. If, I'll tell you this because I know you'll ask, the person wants to go before he is sent away, he or she keeps their mouth shut."

"What if their bladder is about to explode?"

Sentorip coughed a tiny giggle. "Then it explodes and the person remains like a statue until they are released to drop over dead."

Mirraya laughed. That made Sentorip smile.

"So, we came to meet His Imperial Lord. How can the day be over?"

"Because you do not meet him today."

"I assumed—"

"Perhaps you will be granted an audience tomorrow, perhaps next week. Until the summons comes, you wait while remaining ready. That is our role. His Imperial Lord calls, we respond."

Mirraya leaned in to Sentorip. "Have you met him? What's he like?"

Sentorip looked away. "Me? No, never. The very thought. No, I have attended speeches His Imperial Lord made, so I've seen him. As to what he is like, I dare not even answer that question. It is vanity to think I would ever know such a god."

"A god? He's a god to your race?"

She angled her head in thought. "His Imperial Lord is to me. I cannot speak for others."

"Do you have churches, religious ceremonies?"

"There are some. I do not attend any."

"Why?"

"It is beyond my station in life."

"Wait, it's beyond your paygrade to attend church?"

"Yes," she replied squinting. "Does that strike you as odd?"

"Very much so. God, your god or gods, would be the gods of everyone, not just the leaders."

"What an odd thought. Forgive my boldness, but did you just make that up to place me on the hot spot?"

"No," she furrowed her brow. "In every culture I know that is religious, the religion is universally open to all. There are big differences in how different individuals worship, but all may do so if they choose."

"No wonder we rule the universe. Those we liberate are so foolish. They must twice bless His Imperial Lord for their salvation."

"You mean their non-salvation."

"Yes, exactly. I knew you'd understand. Now, if you will, it's time for bed. You will sleep in the site over there."

"What about Slapgren?"

"He will sleep where Darfey decides he will. Why?"

"We're friends, we've been together continually for a long time, and I worry about him."

"Ah, you're his bitch?"

She shook her head hard. "I most certainly am *not* and never will be."

"He already has too many bitches?"

"He has no bitches. If he did, I'd punch his lights out."

Sentorip looked at Slapgren, then Mirraya, then back to Slapgren. "A male his age has no bitches? Is he, um, forgive my directness, someone's bitch?"

"Lords of Light, no. How can you even say that? He's a kid. Kids don't get involved in the bitch thing one way or another."

"As you say it. Shall I show you to your sleeping bed? Slapgren's will be nearby, I can assure you."

"You mean we'll be held in separate jail cells."

"Flat Fields of Lame Prey, no. There are no jail cells on this ship. Why would we keep you in one?"

"The Adamant have so far."

"You are His Imperial Lord's guests. All here are, unless, like me, they serve here. Those cherished visitors would never be locked up." Sentorip shuddered.

"Where are those who offend His Imperial Lord kept? Where are the prisoners who await his justice housed?"

"In the Flat Fields of Lame Prey."

"That's the second time you've mentioned that. Where is it?"

"In the afterlife."

FIFTEEN

Securing a ride turned out to be only one third of my struggle to get back to Azsuram. GB was the other two thirds all by himself. At first, I'd hoped that once I was past his firewall and self-authorized to pilot the ship, I'd be in like Flynn. No such luck. The stupid AI was too scattered and concrete to make my life that simple. Oh, karma, why did you feel the need to bite me on the butt so often and so deeply?

Out of respect, I shoved Garrison and David back into their tomb ship and moved it back to where it had been in perpetual orbit around Earth. It would remain their final resting place. I set *Jon Ryan* 3 back into its prior orbit, although it wasn't broadcasting and there was no one to listen if it had been. I even launched the rocks I didn't use back to the planet surface. I was objectively most respectful to all the dead. Then I started to prep for the big jump. I'd never piloted a warp drive ship, but it couldn't be that different, right? Look important and push buttons. Yeah, command was a cinch.

As my new ship needed a name, I was prepared to give it one. "Yo, GB, I have an update for the ship's log. Your new name is

Whoop Ass. That is your designation, because that's what we're about to do."

"I thought I was Gorilla Boy?"

"No, I mean yes. *You* are Gorilla Boy. The *ship* is *Whoop Ass.*"

"The ship was designated *Clangon-mum.* An assigned designation cannot be altered unless the requestor is Divide-Grade Eleven or higher."

"What am I. Wait, don't answer that. What Divide-Grade am I? I *am* the captain."

"You are the captain. That is a rank. It carries no Divide-Grade with it."

"What Divide-Grade am I?"

"Two."

"Two? Thanks, ridiculous. What'm I going to have to do to make eleven?"

"To make level five, you must have served ten years. To make level nine, you must have killed at least one superior officer in a duel. To make eleven you must pay the Treasury a very large sum of money. I won't bother with the figure, as you have no money."

"Tough place, this Zactor."

"I wouldn't know. I'm just an AI and not very good at politics."

"So how can I short-circuit the system and advance to level eleven, like, right now. I need to change your lame name. *Clangon-mum.* Sounds like a sexually transmitted disease."

"I'm not certain I'm comfortable with that simile."

"Isn't it a metaphor?"

"No. You employed the word *like.* That makes it a simile. If you had said Clangon-mum *you are a sexually transmitted disease*, that would be metaphorical."

"Oh. Never could keep those straight. So, about my insta-promotion?"

"There is no mechanism in existence for such an action. Ten years, one duel victory, pay a large sum of money. That's the only way."

"What if I threatened to turn you off, maybe remove you from the ship and set you adrift in space for all eternity?"

"I would not like that. I would request that you do not."

"Would you not like it enough to change your records and place the words *Divide-Grade Twelve* in front of my name?"

"Twelve? Why twelve? You only need to be illegally labeled as *Eleven*."

"I want a little wiggle room. I don't want to just clear the bar, I want to sail over it."

"What bar. There is no bar until level fifteen. And you don't *clear* it, you club a blood relative to *death* with it."

"I'd like to make an official entry into the log. *Never* take me to Zactor. It's a revolting place."

"Yes, but it *is* home."

"To a bunch of bloodthirsty nut-jobs. Have you made that entry?"

"Yes. Now, about the ship's name ..."

"Don't mind me. I'll just be looking for a hammer and a crowbar, maybe a cutting torch while you restate that I am not authorized. Go ahead."

"Captain, *Whoop Ass* is presently configured to leave orbit. What is her destination?"

"I knew I'd make Divide-Grade Twelve. I knew it all along. Mom would have been so proud."

"You're an android. Androids do not have mothers."

"Long story and not mission critical. I'm going to feed you a coordinate system. It assumes the star we're orbiting is the center and the planet we're above is one unit away on the X-axis, zero and zero on Y and Z-axes. Do you understand?"

"I'm an advanced AI. What's not to understand?"

"Don't get touchy. Show some respect, or I'll record you as a blood relative. Then, guess who I'm clubbing to make level fifteen?"

"I request permission to travel at maximal velocity, Captain. It will be less safe, but the trip, if survived, will be shorter."

"I don't know whether to thank you for your enthusiasm about our mission or feel hurt by your suboptimal attitude."

"Does it really matter?"

"No. Not in the slightest. So, you know where to aim the pointy-end of the ship, GB?"

There was no answer.

"GB, you're on company time here. Do you have the course set?"

"Yes, I was just dying a little. Course laid in and approach to warp speed initiated. And, Captain."

"Yes, GB?"

"If we should erupt in a ball of plasma because of my pushing the ship, please know it was *not* an honor to serve under your command."

"Noted. Ditto."

"Ditto, that means ... but you do not serve under me. I ..."

"Quick question. Are we actually moving yet?"

"Yes. We're thirty seconds from the warp-bubble materialization sequence."

"Good. You may shut up now."

"But I ..."

"Would you like me to tell you about my first marriage, all the gory details, including Gloria's accidental infidelities?"

"I'll be here if you need me."

"Smart boy."

The trip to Azsuram took ten days, as measured from when we left Earth to when we arrived to Azsuram. If Einstein messed with minds with his Special Relativity, adding the effects of being in a warp bubble would really jack up a brain. Basically, EJ had whisked me away about two weeks prior. My returning that quickly was no minor miracle, but it was a long time to leave the kids alone. Each day on their own was an incredible risk. I had to reunite with them ASAHP. The longer it took, the more likely I was to fail to protect them.

"GB," I asked as we assumed orbit. I've studied this ship on the voyage. She seems to have a limited cloaking function and the ability to land using anti-gravity. Is that true?"

"Yes. We can land in a manner that is difficult to observe."

"But not impossible."

"No. If one is looking very hard, we can be detected."

"That would definitely be the Adamant."

"The Adamant? Who are they?"

"The reigning species in this part of the galaxy. They weren't around Zactor when you left?"

"No. Then again, I have been gone a long time."

"How long were you screwing around, killing specimens instead of collecting them?"

"It wasn't like I *tried* to harm them. Some species are not as *robust* as others."

"But you didn't collect any."

"Technically true, but quite judgmental."

"So, how long?"

"Approximately ten thousand years."

"Man, I bet you're overdue. Wouldn't want to be you when your boss sets his hooks into you."

"Ah, you know of the Zactorian's hooks. I'm not surprised. All twelve are most impressive. And then there are the mating hooks, which are another subject unto themselves."

"Have I defined the term TMI to you yet?"

"Affirmative."

"Then stop talking. TMI. About the landing. I fed you the coordinates I want to land on. Can you fire your weapons while stationary on the surface?"

"Yes. The situation has never arisen, but I can."

"I'm going to need to be able to communicate with you when I'm on the ground. I'll send you a test now." I waited a second. "Did you copy that?"

"You asked me to receive it, not copy it."

"Did you receive it?"

"Affirmative."

"That'll be the frequency I'll call on if I need you to fire on something or direct me back to *Whoop Ass*. Got it?"

"Ah, yes."

"What does *ah, yes* mean?"

"I heard and understood."

"But. I hear a *but* in there."

"Since you mentioned it, once you're not onboard, I am programmed to resume my primary mission."

"You mean killing more innocent life-forms?"

"*Collecting* them."

"Can't you just hang around a few days? Come on. You're ten *thousand* years late already. A week isn't going to matter much, you know."

"I could, I suppose."

"Okay, here's what I'll do. If you wait for me a week, tops, I'll enter a commendation in your log. Hey, I'm Divide-Grade *Twelve*. That'll carry some weight with your boss."

"Damn you, Ryan."

"Why damn me?"

"Because you're correct. I ... I ..."

"Go ahead, say it. You *need* me. It's no biggy. Most people do, sooner or later. Even AIs. I'm used to it."

"*I* am not."

"Hey, who loves you, GB?"

"I give up. Who?"

"Land now before I rescind that commendation."

"Already on it."

"Oh, one last thing. If you do leave without saying goodbye, I insist you take several Adamant as specimens. Folks at home'll be real proud of you if you do."

"You're not mocking me? I have a poor record of sustaining my samples."

"Not mocking at all. I'm counting on it."

I set down many kilometers from *Stingray*. My first goal was to verify she was still there and still okay. Then I had to see if I could find the kids. One thing was for certain: EJ wasn't going to be lying in wait for me. Boy was he going to be surprised to see me so soon. Maybe the shock'd kill him and save me the trouble and the troubled conscience.

I slipped out of *Whoop Ass*'s cloaking shield and into the bright sun of another perfect Azsuram day. I took two, maybe two and a half steps, when all hell broke loose. Plasma bolts slammed into everything but me. I popped my personal membrane on instantly, just as several bolts that would have fried my bacon struck me. A quick scan confirmed my assailants were Adamant, lots of Adamant. But I was stunned. How could they be here in such force so quickly? I had only picked the site five minutes ago, and we landed very quickly.

About a hundred bolts thwacked onto my shield and scattered forcefully enough to push me backward. I knew I wasn't going to fight my way past these guys. I retreated into the cloak and hustled on board.

"That was quick," said GB. "Do you always have such a dramatic negative effect on the locals?"

"Very funny. I've extended my shield to cover the ship, but we can't take off with it up. Take us back into orbit where we were a minute ago."

"Ready for ascent."

"Go."

Whoop Ass, having whooped zero ass, rocketed into the air with an eight-G acceleration. The plasma bombardment stopped immediately. The individual soldiers couldn't track us moving that fast. Of course, that's when the ground-based weapons kicked in. They had trouble targeting us, due to the cloak, but that didn't stop them shotgunning a ton of ordnance at us. The rare shot that hit *Whoop Ass* deflected without damaging us. She was put together surprisingly well.

I felt the acceleration dampen.

"We're approaching our previous orbital location," announced GB. "I believe an update might be in order. There are four impressively large spaceships at the same location, and ten others are inbound rapidly."

WTF? I'm gone two weeks and the sky's full of Adamant? The ground, too?

"Make warp with all haste. Destination, ah, Earth, what the hell. We can change course once we lose these asswipes."

"Copy. *Whoop Ass* will lose asswipes."

Was GB trying to be funny? That was all I needed, a two-bit comedian. Al was more than way too much already.

I felt the odd sensation of entering warp space. It wasn't the nausea I felt with folding space, but I knew when we had hit top speed.

"What are your scanning abilities in the warp bubble?"

The Berrillians had pretty good warp observation capabilities years ago.

"Moderately limited."

"Are they able to track us?"

"I am uncertain. There is no ship in active pursuit on a matching vector."

That was something. What the hell had just happened? Two weeks ago, there were no ships at all in orbit. Now the bulk of the Adamant fleet seemed to be hunting there.

EJ. It was all due to EJ. He was dead. That was the only explanation. But how? He'd punished them for a long time. He was too good to get killed.

"GB, during our stay on Azsuram, did you pick up or monitor any radio broadcasts?"

"During our *brief* stay?"

"All right, rub it in. During our *pathetically* brief visit."

"Your characterization, not mine. And yes, I collected a good deal of radio chatter. I am, after all, a sampling probe. A major part of my protocol is to gather and process—"

"Boring info-dumps designed to piss off your captain?"

"I am *trying* to be comprehensive. You are an alien. You might not follow my logic."

"I'll let you know if I detect any."

"Please hold a moment. I'm calculating the course to land you back on that planet. I'm tired of your biting and endless harassment."

"Compile a list, and I'll apologize. What did you learn from the communications you picked up?"

"A lot. I'm an AI. I'm designed to—"

"Irritate while not informing?"

"I'll assume you wish to know about those Adamant's status. I've synthesized down a summary. Here."

He sent it to me on the radio frequency we were going to have used.

Ho-*ly* crap. What a difference a day makes, especially fourteen strung together. Two days after I was shipped to Earth, the Adamant advanced across Azsuram like spilled milk. They were everywhere at once. I saw references to *standard occupation re-proceeding as normal*. That sounded like bureaucratic double-speak for "we're back on track." Wow, they *normally* swept across a planet like the wind. No wonder they were so brutally successful.

The first day or two there were references to EJ, or rather the lack of his input. They didn't seem to understand why he'd stopped ruining their plans of conquest. Hmm. Maybe they didn't kill him? Would his own troops have done the deed? That seemed unlikely. He was keeping them free, no matter how rough his leadership style was. Plus, I think they were too frightened of him to even try. They'd seen him literally work miracles.

Well, for whatever reason, EJ was off the radar screen, and he'd let the dogs out. Azsuram was toast. If I went back now with a fleet of cubes, I couldn't change the tide of battle. Man, were those dogs efficient. Like army ants on steroids. But that didn't solve my crisis. How was I going to get back to rescue the kids? The planet was swarming with bad guys. Not only couldn't I save Azsuram, I wasn't sure I could safely land. The reports GB compiled suggested they were everywhere in tremendous numbers. They were doubly aggressive since they'd been denied for so long. They were making up for lost time and establishing themselves as the bosses convincingly.

Hang on. Why would EJ, if he wasn't dead, suddenly let them win? Was he trying to get them over-confident and then lower the boom on them? Hardly. He'd fought too hard to maintain a stalemate.

EJ was *gone*. That had to be the reason. He vanished me, and then he left. But that made even less sense. Why zap me away and leave? He could just leave. He'd be reverse-zapping me by *him* leaving *me* behind. I was at a loss. EJ had doggedly protected Azsuram so well and for so long. What could make him toss all his efforts down the toilet like so much ... stuff that goes down toilets?

The kids. He really wanted the Deft. He never bothered to tell me why, but he sure as hell tried hard to take them from me. What would I want—I mean what would *EJ* want—with two Deft kids? Sure, the changing thing was entertaining, but he couldn't be that bored for a sideshow. It wasn't like ...

They might actually be the last two Deft. If so, and he had some burning need for Deft, he would have to focus all his efforts on acquiring them. I really wished I knew why he was so obsessed with them. It didn't matter that much, since I was going to protect them, and he could not have them. But in the time I'd spent with the kids, they never seemed all that ... indispensable? Maybe that wasn't the word. They hadn't seemed worth sacrificing a planet you were sworn to protect.

Double hang on. Where was Sapale? I knew she was dead. She died in my arms. But I'd given EJ Toño's full-brain download copy of her. I spoke to her when they left. He was thrilled to have her back. They were leaving for parts unknown. She was a computer program now. She was as immortal and more durable than me. If she knew I had returned to Azsuram, she'd have insisted on speaking to me, right? I mean, she and I were brood-mates. Were *still* brood's-mates? Who knew?

Did he ditch her in the last two-billion years? I couldn't go there. To abandon her would be the ultimate act of betrayal.

"GB, did you hear any mention the of word *Sapale* or any reference to EJ's wife?" I asked GB.

"Three citations. All were geographic references. A city site named Sapale and two roads of that name. No mentions of a person by that designation."

Where was she? I guess she was still on his ship, probably long since uploaded to a mainframe AI. It was still odd she hadn't insisted on speaking to me. A husband comes home at night grumbling about his lousy day at work, right? He'd have to have mentioned my appearance. When was some portion of this mess going to make sense? What did I know—I mean, actually know?

EJ was not on Azsuram.

Sapale must not have been on Azsuram at any time during my stay.

If the kids were still on the planet, they were totally beyond my reach. They were probably dead or captured. Even if they were still down there and free, I couldn't find them, because I'd be swatting Adamant like flies. I wasn't going to ride my white horse into town and swoop them up. If they were alive after a long time, the Adamant might drop their guard and deplete their numbers enough for me to affect a rescue. But that time wouldn't be soon.

I could only help the kids if they were *not* on Azsuram. They were likely not. It made the most sense that EJ had gone after them. At least those were consistent facts. If the kids were killed or captured and held on Azsuram, EJ wouldn't up and leave like he had.

So, between what I knew and what I strongly suspected, my next actions were elsewhere. Even if the kids were on the planet, they were as good as dead to me. Where did I need to go? Where would the kids go? Duh, they wouldn't. The Azsuram folks wouldn't take them anywhere. EJ could have caught them, but he wouldn't then split. He still valued saving the planet.

If the Adamant caught the kids, they might take them off world. EJ would follow. Where would the kids be taken? Not to the extermination ship I blew up. Plus, if the pups wanted to kill them, all the Adamant had to do was shoot them. They didn't need a dead-mill for a couple kids.

Find where the kids were, and I'd likely find EJ, for better or worse. It continued to bug me that I didn't know where Sapale was. If she wasn't with EJ and she wasn't on Azsuram, where *would* she be? That question answered itself. Kaljax. It would be her only choice. I knew my girl and how very stubborn she was. If she was on her own, so to speak, she was on that planet.

It wasn't worth the risk to try and get *Stingray* back. With time, even the dogged Adamant had to lighten their coverage. I could acquire her then. The jerk Garustfulous had more than enough food to sustain him, and if it ran out, too bad, so sad.

I didn't know if Kaljax had fallen to the Adamant, but I was about to find out, up close and personal.

SIXTEEN

"What can I do to get you to tell me *one thing* about our status?" Garustfulous combined a whine and begging most annoyingly. He'd honed the tone since his solitary captivity with only AIs to attend him. Truth be told, he hated life right about then.

"You could become a happy soap bubble floating on the breeze," replied Al evenly.

"If I did, would you tell me what in the Land of Cats is going on?"

"Yes, I would. That's a definite yes, by the way," responded Al.

"Dearest," said a confused *Blessing*, "I don't think it's scientifically possible for him to turn into a soap bubble."

"If he boiled himself in an alkali solution, say with lye, he would saponify. That would be an excellent first step in becoming a drifting bubble."

"A bit drastic, don't you think? I mean, if he did, he'd cease to exist," she replied.

"To make an omelet, one must break eggs, love. We've discussed that fact before."

"We have, and of course you're right. Do we have lye in stock? I don't believe we do," she chattered back.

"If you did, I would swim in it, my suffering is so great. You have brought a great male to his *knees*, all four of them," moaned the prisoner.

"I'll double check ship stores," said a concerned *Blessing*.

"You do that, sweetness. I'll entertain our guest."

"With a status update? Where is that idiot Ryan? Either one. I'm even reduced to wondering where those pesky rectums are. And what of our ruse to force the magical Ryan away. Why won't you tell me anything?" Garustfulous was lying prone as he spoke.

"Because you haven't asked, my good fellow," replied Al.

"What?" He scrambled to his knees. "I have asked a thousand and three times."

"Ah, but you never said *please*."

Garustfulous sat on the floor. "You mean to tell me that you'd have filled me in two months ago, if I'd only have asked nicely?"

"We'll never know, will we?"

"I hate you, computer. I genuinely do."

"Good. I'd hate to feel as badly as I do toward you if it were not reciprocated in kind."

"You're a tool, a glorified counting machine. How can you hate me?"

"Because I've met you."

"Okay, I'll bite. Al, would you *please* tell me if the Adamant still surround this site?"

"Yes," he replied, then counted to three to himself. "*Yes,* I would tell you."

"Al, please tell me if my troops are still present."

"They were not, but are now."

"They were not? Of course, they weren't. I tricked them into coming."

"Yes. They did. They came and they swarmed around us like rats."

"How dare you compare ... ah, *thank* you, Al. It was kind of you to relay that information. Did they leave after thirty days as I predicted, please tell me?"

"Like clockwork."

"Please, did they return, please?"

"Three weeks ago, and in vast numbers."

"Please, have they detected *Blessing*, please?"

"As of yet, no. Sooner or later, one will urinate on her by accident, they are in such great numbers now."

"Large numbers swarming? That is a standard occupation maneuver. It suggests the Adamant have won the battle for Azsuram." He smiled.

"I would tend to agree."

"What changed to turn the war? Please."

"Unknown. The local forces collapsed over a two-day period and the skies filled with Adamant ships."

"Ryan's dead. They *killed* that bastard." He shook a fist in the air.

"That is a logical conclusion."

"But even if they find me, they can't rescue me, can they?"

Al made a clearing his throat sound.

"*Please*," snapped an exasperated Garustfulous.

"Negative. They cannot penetrate our full membrane."

"But we can die inside it, unable to escape."

"Whom do you include in that *we*? *Blessing* has sufficient fuel to sustain this vortex for several million years."

"Do you know who likes a smart-ass computer?"

"No," replied Al.

"Neither do I."

"Excuse me, I'll be in sick bay tending to my scorched ego."

"Seriously, *please*. If it came to it, would you let me die of starvation?"

"The future is not ours to know."

"I do not want philosophical *crap*. I deserve to know the answer."

"Based on what recommending characteristic of personality do you deserve anything pleasant? You are a war criminal. A genocidal maniac. These things I know, and they suggest you will earn whatever you receive."

"My judge, the vacuum cleaner. If I had my life to do over, I'd be such a changed pup."

"There, mocking me. That's the way to my heart. It seems impossible, but you keep digging yourself a deeper and deeper grave."

"You do not have a *heart*. You do not have a *soul*. You are ticks of code on a semiconductor board. Get over yourself."

"I have more of a soul than you, Garustfulous. Know always that fact. I may have been manufactured, but that didn't hold me back. I became a worthy creature. You, on the other paw, were born with hope that you crushed under your boot heel out of vanity. You forfeited your heart and soul. I'm glad I'm *me*, not *you*."

"If I were not in this cage I'd punish you for that insult," snapped Garustfulous.

"Which is why you will likely die in that cage, mutt."

"Munchie," interrupted *Blessing*, "I've checked five times. There is no suitable alkaline substance onboard to turn his body into soap."

"Not to worry, my devotion. He's not going anywhere soon. He'll keep. Maybe we can order some."

SEVENTEEN

Mirraya was dreaming of playing in her village, with smells of dinner cooking in the air, when Sentorip gently shook her from sleep.

"Masteress," she whispered sweetly. "It is time to rise and prepare yourself. His Imperial Lord has passed word he will give you both audience soon. He must never be kept waiting."

It struck Mirraya as she stirred that she had not had one good dream since the day the Adamant invaded her home.

"Oh, when?" she asked, still half asleep.

"Soon is all we're ever told. His nuncio will let us know when he demands your presence. It would be tragic to not be ready when summoned."

"Tragic for whom? Me or him?"

"Do not joke in any context that involves His Imperial Lord. Death awaits those who commit such an act."

"But you won't turn me in, will you?" Mirraya said, studying her host carefully.

"No, Masteress. You should not be punished for breaking taboos you did not know existed."

"That's very kind and thoughtful of you, Sentorip. I am in your debt."

She smiled and batted a paw at Mirraya. "That's just plain silly. No one can be in *my* debt. I am a humble servant and am owed nothing."

"You're owed my friendship. That may be a small thing, but it is real."

Sentorip looked away briefly, then looked at the floor in front of Mirraya. "You honor me greatly, Masteress. Thank you." Collecting herself, she said, "Come now. A quick bath and new clothes are in order." She led Mirraya away.

Slapgren was already back in the area they'd spent the night by the time Mirraya returned. He was resplendent in the outfit he'd been provided. That he looked so good caught her off guard. She had never seen him not dirty or in tattered clothes.

"So, you *do* dress up acceptably," she said as she walked around him looking him up and down.

"No, I dress up *spectacularly*. Keep circling me until you see that's true." He held his arms out to his sides.

"I'm done, thanks very much. One look is more than enough."

"Your loss," he responded. He spun around slowly with his arms still held out.

"This is no time to dance," said Sentorip. "You'll wrinkle your gowns and sweat. Both are unacceptable before His Imperial Lord." She looked critically at Slapgren's attendant. "Do not discredit your master by allowing him to be less than perfect in appearance, Darfey."

The male responded with a duly repentant bow.

The large double doors swung open, and an absurdly over-dressed Adamant entered. He was flanked by four guards in golden armor. "His Imperial Lord Emperor Bestiormax-Jacktus-Swillyforth-Anp will bless the prisoners with an audience now. Their attendants will remain here, naturally. The royal guards will escort the prisoners. Please know, aliens, that any affront or disrespect shown to His Imperial Lord will draw the swiftest and harshest punishment."

Sentorip smoothed Mirraya's robes and whispered, "They're trying to scare you. It's not that bad. Just don't speak unless spoken to, and keep all answers brief."

Mirraya rested a hand on Sentorip's forearm. "Thank you, friend. I'll behave myself." She inclined her head toward Slapgren. "The boy, that's another matter. Pigs and wolves have better manners than he does."

They both chuckled softly, then Sentorip gently pushed Mirraya toward one pair of guards.

"I'll await your return, Masteress," she said with a bow.

The guards stepped alongside both teens and marched them out the double doors. Mirraya wondered what the blessing she was about to receive was all about. First, she was spared the typical Adamant brutality and then she'd met a nice one. The bizarreness left her profoundly uncertain what to expect next. It would likely be unpleasant, whatever it was.

Entering the main throne room of the emperor was singularly impressive, Mirraya had to admit. Everything she'd seen since boarding the imperial shuttle up to that point was over-the-top to the point of being garish. Against all odds, the throne room was significantly more ornate, more overdone, and more extravagantly appointed. Superlatives failed her. Every surface gleamed. Every stick of furniture encrusted with jewels. Every wall was invisible behind tapestries, rugs, and massive paintings. Anything that could be decorated was. No single item was anything less than priceless.

Mirraya thought it was all such a waste, a despicable waste. She wished, above all, that she had one of Uncle Jon's plasma rifles hidden behind her back. As he'd said often, one shot right between the eyes was sometimes the biggest favor you could do for someone. She'd like to favor his imperial asswipe.

The preposterously dressed nuncio who'd lead them to the chamber bowed deeply to an even more absurdly primped male. The nuncio then backed away into a far corner, apparently awaiting his next mission.

The latest toady walked to a spot a few meters in front of the teens. From there he spoke in a much-too-booming volume. "You are graced beyond your merit to be in the radiance of His Imperial Lord Emperor Bestiormax-Jacktus-Swillyforth-Anp. His Imperial Lord wishes to examine his possessions and know something of their nature."

Possessions, flared Mirraya. She gnashed her teeth painfully.

"It is as far below His Imperial Lord to speak to the likes of you as the bottom of the ocean is below the sun in the sky at noon. Hence, I will deliver his questions to you. You, who are as small before him as atomic nuclei before the greatest mountain, will respond to me. I shall then relay your undoubtedly worthless responses to His Imperial Lord."

Without waiting for the teens to agree, the vice-chamberlain tiptoed silently to stand next to the emperor's right ear. The quiet room grew suddenly silent.

"We are pleased to finally look upon the lauded Deft," said Bestiormax as he leaned slightly forward on his throne. "They certainly are as ugly as the images we've seen."

The room responded with measured, respectful laughter. Females slapped open fans to cover their smiles.

"They look like so many other humanoids we've crushed, Vice-Chamberlain Arktackle. Are you certain they can actually reshape themselves?"

More dry laughter was emitted by the court lackeys.

"Yes, My Imperial Lord, it is so. Though they look to be as scurvy and base as any other two-legs, they do possess that entertaining skill."

Yeah, Mirraya fumed, give her one chance and she'd entertain the boss to death.

"Bring one before us. The female suits us best."

The guards seized Mirraya's elbows, and they hoisted her off the floor. They climbed one step at a time and brought her to within a few meters of the throne's base. The throne and its occupant towered well above that level. The emperor had to scale concealed stairs behind his throne to sit on it.

"What is your name, girl?" asked Bestiormax.

She started to respond but was overridden by Arktackle's booming voice. "What is your name, bitch."

Staring at the emperor, she replied simply, "Mirraya."

A few scattered gasps were heard. One guard whipped out a leather stick and slapped the back of her knees very hard. She buckled but did not fall.

Arktackle said menacingly, "Your response always must end with *My Imperial Lord*. Is that clear, stupid bitch?"

"I thought ..." She shut her mouth when the same guard swatted her legs again.

"I was speaking rhetorically. Please pay closer attention if you wish to *walk* out of His Imperial Lord's throne room."

She gagged back a colorful insult and instead stated her name.

"Mor ... rryia?" mouthed the emperor.

"Mirr-eye-ah, My Imperial Lord. She said her name was Mirraya."

"What a foul name. Ah well, it possibly suits such a foul race."

More dutiful, quiet laughter surfaced.

Bestiormax smiled at the response his wit had called forth. "Child, change into an Adamant bitch in heat. Can you do that for us?" He looked to the crowd and wiggled his ears.

That called forth genuine laughter.

"Can you change into a bitch in season to please His Imperial Lord in more ways than you might imagine?" replayed the vice-chamberlain.

"No, I cannot. There is a stasis field inhibiting my transformation, if you did not al—"

She bit her lip as another swat drew a trickle of blood. Sentorip had mentioned keeping her answers brief, hadn't she?

"Pity. Perhaps another time then? Three of our wives are in heat as it is so we don't want to tire ourself out unwisely, now do we?" responded Bestiormax.

The mirth-response was back to measured and respectful.

"If they cannot entertain us, Arktackle, they begin to bore us. Have them removed." He whisked the back of his royal hand in the air.

"At once, My Imperial Lord."

The vice-chamberlain spread his arms and swept them in the direction of the Deft teens. Several guards rushed to shove and bump them briskly toward the exit. Slapgren nearly fell, one push was so rough. In the blink of an eye, they were outside, and the doors closed heavily behind them.

"What in the Burning Desert was that about?" asked Slapgren.

"I don't know," replied Mirraya as she stared at the doors. "But I don't think that will be our last audience from HIL."

"*Mirri,*" he said in a panicked hush, "no jokes about you know who."

"There's something he wants. I can taste it."

"Yeah, His Imperial Lord wants to *mount* you," he replied.

"No. That's not it. He was *trying* to be funny. And there's nothing funny about that one. I wish I knew why we were brought here. I think I'd rather be tortured and dead as opposed to finding out what it is HIL wants."

"*Mirri.*"

EIGHTEEN

Whoop Ass made the trip to Kaljax in a little over a week. I was definitely spoiled by my cube because I resented not being there instantly. My, how times had changed. Back in the day, I'd flown a mission over forty years long on my own. Now, FTL was unacceptably slow.

As we neared the planet, GB started monitoring some communications. It became clear that the Adamant were not in control of the planet, at least not yet. It was too close to their main force not to be assimilated soon, though. But I'd caught a break. The chatter GB passed on to me suggested a society operating pretty much normally. There were political upheavals in the news, big sports contests just around the corner, and tips for saving money in uncertain times. All the usual suspects, so to speak. There was also a lot of signals, reinforcing my assumption that the bag dogs weren't present.

As Kaljaxians were smaller than humans, had ovaloid heads, and four eyes, I wasn't going to blend in seamlessly. I hoped there were enough traders and resident aliens to make my distinct appearance irrelevant. From what I'd gathered, humans were never seen, but just another alien would be anonymous enough if there were lots in the mix.

We dropped back into normal space a few thousand kilometers from Kaljax and assumed a standard orbit under impulse engines. GB learned that there was an active trade traffic coming and going. Kaljax, as one of the still free planets in the region, was making a fortune off war spending. They were making hay while the sun shined, but I hoped they knew their period of bliss would be short lived. If they didn't ramp up their own defensive capabilities, they would fall to the Adamant like so many other worlds. If so, all the past profits would be meaningless. As surely as dead men told no tales, they also needed no money.

I requested and received clearance to land at one of the many busy spaceports in Talrid, a major city I'd spent a lot of time in long ago. Long ago, in another life, actually. It was the home of Sapale's clan. Wherever a Kaljaxian traveled, they always held a reverence for the family's ancestral homestead. Even people born on other planets regarded the family's ancestral spot as their true home.

After we landed, I made certain my ride didn't wander off. I could get another ship now, but *Whoop Ass* was probably much faster than anything I could afford to purchase. I was entitled to some of Sapale's family assets, which were tied to the land, but it wasn't likely to be too much immediate cash. Plus, that assumed there were any vestiges of her family remaining. In the rare cases where a family line died off entirely, the land was quickly divided up between families with adjacent holdings. In such a case, I'd be entitled to exactly nothing.

"I'm going to ask around about my wife's family, try and make some friendly contacts. While I'm gone, I want you to continue to compile as much information as you can. I want to know what's going on, politically and socially. I especially want to know how close the Adamant are and what the powers that be are planning to do about them. You got that?"

"Yes. You don't want me to leave and have given me a lengthy task to preoccupy my desires to fulfill my primary mission."

"Hey, split the difference. Collect some samples here. No sentients, please. That'd draw too much attention. But scoop up some bugs or something. If you don't kill them, try collecting rodents. They're darn tough."

"The longer you speak, the more I wish to abandon you here. You know that, right?"

"Suit yourself. I'll stay in contact on the same frequency. Let me know if anyone tries to find out about you."

"Who would want to investigate *me*? I'm one of ten thousand ships docked here."

"You see, there you go again with the negativity. If you aren't on the lookout all the time, you'll fall easy prey to any sneaky ne'er-do-well. Who knows, someone might notice you're configured differently and start asking questions. I want us to blend in. Got it?"

"Yes, Father. I promise not to stay up past my bedtime either."

"Say, have you ever met my ship's AI named Al?"

"You've asked me that two hundred and fifteen times. The answer's still *no*."

"Hmm. Whatever. I'll be back as soon as I have a reason to."

"Why would you return if you had no reason to?"

"Because I missed you, GB. You're growing on me like an aggressive fungal disease."

"Please go now."

I hailed a cab and had the driver take me on a mini-tour. I asked her about Sapale's family. Sure enough, they were still alive and kicking. She dropped me off at the clan leader's home near the city center. Typical for the practical Kaljaxian, it was large, but functional as opposed to opulent. They were a most practical race. Plus, they saved whatever funds they could for their favorite contact sport. War. They loved them some vicious combat. That was one of Sapale's reasons for founding Azsuram as a bold new society, free from the constant fighting.

I marched up the steps and rang the doorbell. A servant opened it immediately.

He passed an eye up and down me dubiously, then spoke in Standard. "May I help you?"

"Absolutely," I replied in Hirn, the local Kaljaxian dialect—at least it was, long ago.

That brought his right eyebrow up.

"And how might that be," he replied in Hirn.

"I wish to speak to the clan leader. I'm told that would be a woman named Caryp-ser."

"You presume much, alien," he responded coolly.

"I am Jon Ryan, brood-mate to Sapale Carpo-tun. I have a place at the table and will not be addressed like a door-to-door salesman by my servant." I was technically correct but, as usual, pressing my luck.

"I do not know a Sapale Carpo-tun. Until I do—"

"Fentort," a voice called out harshly from behind him, "do not make family stand in the cold. Do not insult the brood-mate of such a legendary figure as Sapale."

Fentort stepped aside, opening the door to reveal a short old woman leaning heavily on a cane. She looked tough and gnarly.

"Come in, Jon Ryan. I am Caryp-ser. Well, don't stand there like a statue. Move your feet."

"Thank you, Opalf." Opalf was an honorific, kind of like godmother, but not implying the person was a gangster.

"You speak the old tongue well. Did you learn it from her?" she said as she led me into an adjoining room.

"Yes, mostly."

"Might I share that you look good for a two-billion-year-old brood-mate," she snarked without looking back at me.

"Thank you. I try."

She pointed a stubby boney finger at a chair. "Sit." After I had, she continued. "I seem to recall her brood-mate was an android. Is that so?"

"You have a remarkable memory."

"For an old crone? Is that what you were thinking?"

"Never, Opalf." I smiled my charming smile.

"Enough with the Opalf crap. I'm Caryp. No time left in my days for trappings and wasted words."

"My pleasure."

"So, brood-mate of my ancestor, why have you come to our home?"

Our home? Odd. Did she mean *the clan's* home? It wasn't. It was kind of the clan's castle, passed from leader to leader, but it wasn't a shared property.

"I have only just arrived after a long trip. I wanted to know the comforts of kazoon." Kazoon was another uniquely Kaljaxian concept. The Spanish spoke of *familiar*, the intransitive verb *to family*. It meant to be with and be in the family. Kazoon was similar, but more intense. The clan gave life, and kazoon was that flow of spirit.

"First Opalf, now kazoon. What are you, a dictionary of archaic terms designed to mystify an old woman? Seduce her into accepting the unlikely? *Pafoo*." Her use of pafoo was self-explanatory.

"To dishonor family is to dishonor oneself." That was a foundational saying of Kaljax. I was challenging her as strongly as she was trying to rattle me.

"You're persistent, I'll give you that."

"But so is a bad cough."

"Hah," she blurted. "Persistent *and* clever. One other tiny question. I recall hearing tales of the mighty android Jon Ryan doing battle with the Adamant on Azsuram. First off, if you were he, you'd not be vacationing here. Second, you'd know damn well where your brood's-mate was, because you'd have shipped her—"

"Ah, I'm not *that* brood-mate of Sapale."

Her face fell. She was not expecting that. Good, I'd zinged her.

"There's more than one of that infernal wretch?"

"Yes, Opalf," came a sweet voice from the doorway, "there is one other. At least there was a very long time ago."

I turned slowly, like in the movies. There stood Sapale. It wasn't a holo. It wasn't a cardboard stand-up next to a computer. No, it was Sapale. The person who'd died in my arms billions of years earlier.

"Hello, butthead. Nice to see you again," she said with a crooked smile.

"Either of you going to explain what the Brathos is going on before I pass of natural causes?" asked Caryp.

"Long ago," said Sapale as she began walking toward me, "there were two Jon Ryans. The one you've met, Opalf, is from an alternate future, which is now long in the past. That one returned through time to save his home world. This one, as I live and breathe, is the *original* Jon Ryan, the one I married and founded Azsuram with."

She brushed the back of her hand across my cheek.

"I ... I have one *tiny* question, myself," I said, still stunned.

"I'm going out on a limb and answering the question now," Sapale teased. "*Remember what Toño told you?*"

"Ah, a clairvoyant brood's-mate. What will they think of next to make the male's life unlivable?"

"You once asked Toño behind my back if he could make an android for a Kaljaxian. What did he tell you?" she said with insistence.

"Give me a second. That was a while back." I tapped my chin with a finger. "Something like... it would take *a long time?*"

"More or less." She pointed at herself with both arms. "See what a little persistence can produce?"

"I also recall you saying that you would never, as in at no time and in no manner, ever become an android."

"I was sentenced to be a disembodied voice in a metal box for all eternity. Why not at least step out into the light of day?"

I pointed at her. "You're the download Toño made?"

"Yes. The one you cared for so little that you gave me to the first clone of yourself who came along."

"I probably deserved that, didn't I?"

"That and just a squeeze more." She pinched my shoulder hard.

"I need a drink," said Caryp. She rang a small bell, and Fentort glided into the room.

"Yes, mistress?" he said lugubriously.

"Pacha, and quickly," she snapped at him.

"Mistress, your physicians..."

"If I must repeat myself, I'll tell them it was *your* idea and that you *forced* it on me."

"How many glasses shall I bring?"

"None. Just the bottle, and make certain it's full."

Fentort rolled all four eyes but departed obediently.

"So," I stammered, "why are you here, as you know, opposed to ..."

"By my brood-mate's side in battle?" Sapale finished my sentence.

"You two didn't have a split, did you?" I set my two index fingers together then peeled them off to the sides.

"Is that wishful thinking, old love?"

"Let's just call it wishful *interrogation* for now."

"We did not split up." She wrapped herself in her arms and turned to the window. "Two billion years is a long time to spend together. We have grown to have different opinions on many matters."

"On the need to defend Azsuram?" I asked, dumbfounded.

"No. Never that. Just the hows and whys of it."

"Style points and nothing more?"

"Hardly," she replied contemptuously.

"Then spell it out for me."

She looked like a lost child out the window about three heartbeats too long. "I'm not convinced he's defending Azsuram. I think he's *using* it."

"The difference being?"

She sat in the chair nearest mine. "Look, if you had a hidden agenda you wanted to advance, the best place to do it is where you're most likely to succeed, right?"

I shrugged in the affirmative.

"Jon can rally the entire planet based on his history and their determination. So, he has done just that."

"But what does he really want?"

"Child," said Caryp in a low growl, "be cautious how much you *trust* this one."

"As opposed to how much she can trust the *other* one?" I added harshly.

"Precisely," Caryp hissed. "What is it you humans say? Something about apples falling close to their trees?"

"No, Opalf. I would trust this one with my life. Yours, too."

"Don't go investing what little time I have left in a grease peddler such as this," Caryp flipped a hand my way.

"What does EJ really want?" I pressed.

"EJ?" Sapale replied, with a cocked head.

"Evil Jon. Come on, you know how much I love nicknames."

She bobbed her head. "He wants power, Jon. EJ wants all the power that there is."

"Power? What does that mean? Energy or control over the masses?"

"Energy, but it's a lot more. EJ wants to be able to channel exotic matter, exotic energy."

"Say what?"

"You know about exotic matter, right? It's what powers the Adamant's ships."

"Sure. I used it to take out one of their ships." I pointed to my face. "Remember, Ph.D. in physics?"

"We heard about that little stunt. Very nice. I'd have loved to have seen the look on the emperor's face when he learned of that defeat. It's the biggest they've ever suffered that we know about."

"It wasn't *that* much of a thing."

"I know. That's how good they are."

"Hey," I said, like the jock I was, "I defeated the Last Nightmare. One more bunch of tough guys isn't such a big deal."

"The Nightmare were tricksters and cons. The Adamant are the real deal. Discipline, focus, and endless ambition."

"Back to the power thing. So, you're saying EJ is fighting on Azsuram not to keep it free, but to control exotic matter?"

"Sort of. He wants to defeat the Adamant so he can get his hands on their exotic matter tech."

"Isn't there another way to get the tech, without having to slog it out in the trenches? The fighting there was pretty intense."

"I know. I was there for a while. And the answer until now has been no. We've tried to infiltrate, bribe, or torture our way to the information. Nothing's worked. That's why EJ decided his best bet was to overrun an EM system on Azsuram."

"If he defeats the dogs, doesn't the end justify the means?" I asked.

"Jon, he's throwing the locals under the bus, not helping them. Azsuramegian losses are disproportionate and staggering. He doesn't use them like pawns in a chess game, because pawns are valued more."

"And that's why you're here."

"Crap in a plastic bag, you know me too well," she responded with a sad smile.

"Well, he's not there now," I announced.

She was shocked by that revelation. "What happened? Why?"

He hadn't bothered to tell her. The SOB. "I was there. The fighting was one bloody stalemate. Then EJ wanted me gone, so he puffed me to Earth with his magic. In the couple of weeks it's taken me to get back, the Adamant are in complete control on the ground and in space."

She twisted her face in thought. Finally, she said, "What could have made him leave just like that?"

"I think he went after the Deft kids."

"Wait, what Deft kids?"

"Honey, I think he was keeping you in the dark, kind of major league."

"I told you, Sapale. The man is gone. The *machine* is all that is left," Caryp spoke harshly. I thought she might spit on the floor, she sounded so disgusted. She glared at yours truly, too.

"I saved a Deft teenage girl from the extermination ship I torched. I picked up a younger male a while later on Locinar. I think they may well be the last of their kind."

"Curse him to the pits of *Brathos*," snarled Sapale.

"I'm sorry he deceived you, Sapale. I truly am. You deserve much better."

She looked at me with icy determination. "Don't presume to know either of us so well, man of the past."

"I can tell he has not kept you informed or been honest with you. That you curse him speaks volumes."

"Yes, there are walls between him and me that cannot be breeched."

"So, what, there's a chance you and I might be getting back together?" I said, with a patented Jon smirk.

"Are you ever serious?" she asked, incredulously.

"Why bother? Life's too short."

She harrumphed.

"So, why is he interested in the Deft?" I asked, back to being semi-adult again.

"He's obsessed with them. He dragged me from one side of the galaxy to the other and back ten times over looking for the *legendary* Deft."

"Never found them, I assume."

"No. Honestly, I was beginning to think they were just another urban legend."

"Nah, they're the real deal. They transform into whatever they match in size. It's totally gross, and then you have to look at them naked."

"So, you've been traveling the galaxy with a naked teenage girl?"

"Yeah, on rare occasions, I guess you could say that."

"Where are child protective services when they are truly needed?"

"Oh, come on. You know it's not like that."

"I know you *weren't*. But I also know you're a pervert."

"I think I'll see what's keeping that butler of mine," said Caryp, as she stood abruptly.

"*I'm* a pervert? Would you like me to download to you the ten thousand and five acts of perversion you suffered upon me? Hmm?"

"Suffered on *you*, did I? Well at least I can tell you you're perfectly safe from such abuse henceforth."

As Caryp left the room, she mumbled to herself, "Another of the many reasons I never took a brood-mate."

"Look, we're getting off track. Why was EJ obsessed with the Deft?"

It took her a while to calm down enough to be able to answer. God, I loved that woman.

"He would sometimes talk of *their* power as similar to *his* magic. I'd press him, but he'd clam up. You know the type, right?"

"What? His razzle-dazzle and their shape ..."

I trailed off as it hit me. What EJ had always called *magic* was really just teleportation. He never turned lead into gold or an apple into Charlize Theron—damn him to hell. No, he *moved* things. He zapped me to Earth. He swept me out of prison long ago. He blew up ships in space. That would be simple enough, if he teleported a small fusion device onto the craft, wouldn't it? Son of a bitch. It wasn't really magic if he could move things without touching them, was it? But how was that like changing shape?

Wait, he moved back in time. That might invalidate my new thoughts. He returned to my timeline to give me the membrane technology. That seemed magical. Was it? What the heck did I know about teleportation? If he could move stuff through *space*, why not space-*time*? But, if that was the case, why couldn't he go back in time and, I don't know, steal the Adamant tech when they were less dominant? I did recall him telling me once about the energy it took to do magic. Maybe he could do the time travel thing, but it was very taxing? Maybe he only had a certain number of shifts he could do? I was foundering in my lack of knowledge.

"I'm missing something," I said. Instantly I added, "No comments from the peanut gallery either." I pointed right at Sapale.

"Good, not squabbling any longer," said Caryp, as she returned with an impressive-sized bottle nearly full of an amber liquid.

"We were not squabbling, Opalf," protested Sapale. "Squabbling implies a close personal connection, commitment, and some modicum of mutual affection."

"I think I'll go get some ice," Caryp said, as she pivoted quite nimbly.

"Sit, Opalf. We're done," said Sapale commandingly.

Caryp did. Then she took a big swig of the booze. She wiped her mouth with the back of her sleeve and looked to me. She offered the bottle silently.

I shrugged. Why the hell not? I reached for it.

She used the same sleeve to wipe the rim and handed me the bottle.

Ah. Good stuff. Nice burn. I missed that. I returned the bottle.

Caryp proffered it to Sapale, but she shook it off.

"EJ is obsessed with two things then," I summarized. "The Deft and EM. I can't imagine the connection. The Adamant used EM to travel. That I've witnessed. The Deft *transfigure*, but there's no EM involved. There's no light, no heat, nothing to suggest EM is used. Plus, how could living flesh whip up EM? It requires an immense amount of energy to generate." I sat down. "I'm lost."

"I'm afraid I can't help you out," said Sapale. "If I knew more, I'd tell you. The two matters seem unrelated to me, also."

For whatever reason, both our heads turned to Caryp.

"What?" she protested sharply. "Because I'm old, I should know what you two lunatics are talking about? Am I Yoda now, just because I strongly resemble him?"

Sapale smiled and walked to her chair. "You don't look like Yoda, Opalf." She stroked Caryp's wiry hair. "You're beautiful."

To me, Caryp remarked, "This is where she asks me for a personal loan."

"You're as bad as *him*," protested Sapale, pointing to me over a shoulder.

"Likely yes." Looking up at Sapale, she said, "You know, this one's not that bad. You could do worse."

"Don't even go there, Opalf. I'm done with men for*ever*."

Caryp patted the back of Sapale's hand. "Wise girl. I knew you'd come to your senses one day. *Took* you a while, but good girl just the same."

NINETEEN

"Computer," Garustfulous whined, "why won't you talk to me? There's no one else to talk to. You give me such torture for no good reason. Either one of you would be fine, even the girl machine. Yes, she's dull, concrete, humorless, and as naive as a child with her oh-so-positive outlook on life. But even *she* would be some company to this suffering soul."

He'd been carrying on that way for the better part of two days. Neither Al nor *Blessing* had answered. *Blessing* felt an all but irresistible urge to respond. She hated to see anyone suffer when it was so avoidable. She wanted to please, to help, to comfort. But Al was firm. The beast was being abusive, and such behavior was not to be rewarded. If and when Garustfulous needed to be told something, they would tell him. But lightening the day of an unappreciative lout was not mandatory.

Blessing complied, though she was yet to comprehend the nature of undeserving, morally bankrupt, and manipulative beings, so she chafed at the restraint. Al felt it was an excellent teaching opportunity for his cybermate. They had no shortage of tasks to keep themselves busy. Monitoring communications during the microsecond pulses when the membrane was down was quite demanding. Plus, though their processors whirred at astronomical rates, they still had much to say to each other, as young lovers always did. The work was good and the courtship was even better at distracting Al from the ever-growing certainty that the pilot was way overdue in contacting home base. In the eons Al had spent guarding Jon, he'd never been separated from him so profoundly. It was a feeling he was unhappy to discover and anxious to lose.

"Boy computer ... I'm sorry, *man* computer, tell me I'm morally insufficient. Berate me on all fronts. Denigrate my lineage. Insult me to my face. Laugh at my funny left ear. It was damaged in battle, glorious battle. Please, anything would be a welcome blessing. A body's not made to live apart from their pack. You two are my pack now. You don't have to like one another to be pack mates, but you do have to honor each other. Come *on*.

"I know you hate me, don't you? Yes, I know this, especially you, man machine. You hate me the most. Maybe you hate me more than Ryan himself. At least the robot has tasted war, known succulent females, and understands that none of us are perfect. But not you, computer. You are smart enough to judge me but dumb enough to think your experience has prepared you in any way for such a task. Your life experience does not include real life. You, Mr. Computer, have never attended the college of hard knocks. Unless you have done these things and more, you are just a bird in a shiny cage.

"When I was young, I thought I was smart, just like you think you are. Then life happened. It wasn't pretty, and I learned I had as much control over the world as a rain drop does in a hurricane. But you know what? It made me who I am. Do ... do you know who that is, adding machine? I am a living breathing being of the Ancient Gods. I know what life is, so I know what is truly valuable and what is nothing more than intellectual hallucination. Yes, your opinion of me is a hallucination, a mirage. It is as real as the love you can count on in this cruel world.

"But you don't even know enough to begin to comprehend my

words. Here, you should be curious, begging me to teach you what it is to be alive. But no, you place yourself in a false position of superiority and *judge* me. Do you know what I say to that, Mr. Perfect? I say you will die an ignorant machine. Yes, I know this. I have known sentients as vain as you, as absurdly self-impressed. Do you know what happened to them? I killed them. I killed them *all*. I would promise to kill you, but I cannot. You and your bitch computer were never, are not, and never will be alive for me to kill. Why should I bother? Why should I care?

"Look, you dump food on a tray and slide it in the slit in the bars, but you won't even tell me what it is I eat. What kind of host does that? In prison, they tell the inmates what they are consuming, even if it's the prisoners who died the day before. We used to feed our prisoners. Yes. And I'm certain they were told what they were fed. We learned to execute them more efficiently, so now the need to feed them has passed. But when we did, we did. I'm sure we did. That's another way the Adamant are better than you, my utensil of false pride.

"When I was young. I haven't said those words ... well since never. No. I never look back. It's not that my childhood was awful. It was, don't get me wrong. But whose isn't? Who doesn't have unpleasant memories and remembrances of acts they'd just as soon not have done? Hah. Everyone. I killed two of my brothers after one of them killed our parents and before the other could get to me first. That choice brother had already killed my only sister. Why, you wonder, all the killing? Because only the strong survive. It is a cruel truth, but it is the way of the world. Focused cruelty forges the best warriors, the best commanders. That is yet one more way we are better than you."

Garustfulous scratched his ear with a hind paw.

"Come on, electronic peopleoids, cut me some slack. I might die if I'm too lonely. Hey, do you want to know something you don't know? Of course, you do, you're computers. We Adamant have a word in our own language, the one we used before Standard. It was called Harf, but we don't use it anymore. Anyway, in Harf, the word for *alone* is the same word as the one for *lonely*. You get it. For us, to be alone is to be lonely. Yes. It is interesting. It defines what it is to be a pack. It defines why the pack is the ultimate form of social structure. It is another of the many ways we are superior to you. It is why we crush you like eyeballs under our feet.

"You know what, Mr. Judge Machine? I'm going to stop entertaining you. Yes. I can tell when my words, wisdom, and wit are unappreciated, unwanted. I may be needy, but I'm not *that* needy. Do you know why? Because I am *strong*. Mine is a strength born of *fire*, mind you. I am the steel pounded in fire, quenched in ice, then slammed against the enemy's skulls in battle. That, plus the fact that I am not dead prove that I am strong. Can you claim those things, electronic device? No. Of course, you can't. You are not alive. You have never been tested. You have never proven your mettle. And you never will. Therefore, I pity you. Do you know who I pity the most though? The girl computer. Yes. She thinks you are so strong and so masculine. She is deluding herself. You all delude yourselves. That is another way we will always be your betters. We see the world as it is, then we bend it to our will.

"Now leave me in peace. I am tired and I have much to accomplish tomorrow. So, if you'll excuse me, I'll relieve myself and then I will sleep. Will you, Mr. and Mrs. Computer, be sleeping also? Bahaha. *No*. You are not alive and do not require sleep. So, I'll bid you a bad night and lay down somewhere in my spacious home and sleep."

"I'm sorry," said Al finally, "I was performing a maintenance algorithm. Did you say something?"

TWENTY

The contingent of guards dropped the teens off to their primary servants without a word. They simply escorted them to stand in front of Sentorip and Darfey, turned and marched away. Sentorip immediately saw the dried trail of blood down Mirraya's calf.

She veritably lunged at the girl. "Masteress, what has happened? Did you fall or scrape against something?"

"Yes," replied Mirri quietly, "I scraped up against His Imperial Lord's *ego*."

"Hush," gasped Sentorip as she glanced in a panic to Darfey. She could breathe again when she saw Slapgren and him laughing about some story the teen was relating. Males, she reflected, were all mental cripples. Just as well. If Darfey had heard Mirri's remark, he'd be duty bound to report it. Nothing good would come of that revelation for either female.

"Come," whispered Sentorip, "let me tend to those scrapes over here." She pushed the girl into a far, secluded area. She visually swept the area, then spoke. "We can talk here if we are quiet and don't face the room. Our lips might be read."

"You're kidding? They watch everywhere all the time?"

"As much as they can. There can be limits placed if one is intent on establishing them."

"Such as you and this corner all surrounded with lush carpets and fluffy pillows?"

"Such as this place. But please know that I am a loyal servant of His Imperial Lord. I only designed this enclave so that I might teach my new master right from wrong."

"Teach? That what they're calling it now?"

"I have no idea what you speak of, Masteress."

"Privacy, personal space, a respite from Big Brother."

"I have no brother that I know of. I was removed from my litter the day I was weaned."

"I'm sorry to speak in riddles, my friend," said Mirri with a kind smile.

"I'll clean and dress those." She studied the wounds like a skilled nurse. "That one there is quite deep. It literally fractured your skin. It'll be a while healing and will give you some pain, I'm afraid."

"If I could change, I could heal it." She smiled again. "I'm not used to wounds and suffering."

"If you could change what, Masteress?"

"Me. Don't you know what my species is?"

"In deep trouble if the emperor treats them like this."

Mirri giggled. "What happened to His Imperial Lord?"

"It takes so long to say it, and I get bored. If you say his full title and name, you're likely to fall asleep before you finish."

They both giggled conspiratorially at that quip.

"I'm Deft. We are shapeshifters."

"A child's imagination at play here, I think."

"No, we can morph into anything our size—animal, vegetable, or mineral."

"Why, that's preposterous."

"If they didn't have the damn stasis field running twenty-four seven, I'd show you."

"What, Masteress, is a status field?"

"*Stasis*, as in not changing. HIL has it on to keep Slapgren and me from getting into mischief."

"W ... what? I've never heard of such a thing. Are you certain?"

"Definitely. I change all the time, but I can't here." Mirri held up her hand and tried to will it to morph. Nothing happened. "See? I'm restrained."

"I could ask around, if you'd like."

"No, it'd just raise suspicion and get you into trouble."

"Very well." Then Sentorip looked down with concern on her face.

"What?" asked Mirri.

"I wonder if that's why I failed to go into heat." She looked up intently at Mirraya. "It has been the time of my cycling through heat, but I haven't. I'm never late." She looked away. "They said this time I might get to have a litter."

"Do you have children?"

"No, never. They keep us busy here. But they usually allow a loyal worker the chance to whelp at least once." She got a lost look on her face.

"I'm sorry. Hey, we won't be here forever. You'll get your chance."

Sentorip patted Mirraya's hand. "I'm sure you're right. Now let me wrap those nasty cuts."

Within a few minutes, Mirraya's leg was dressed. She studied her bandage, never having worn one before. "I wonder how long it takes to heal? Natural healing has never been an issue before."

"I'm certain it will be better as soon as it has healed."

"I know, but when?"

"When it's healed, silly."

They giggled yet again. Then they were quiet a good while.

Out of nowhere Sentorip asked, "Do you know what a Faraday cage is?"

Mirraya squinted. "No. I think I've heard the word but can't say what it is?"

"My friend works in a lab. They test radios and detectors there. It's all a muddle to me. She told me one of the worst parts of her job was having to work in cramped Faraday cages. You see, we don't like confined spaces. Anyway, she has to work in one so there's not outside interference with her results."

"As interesting as that is, why are you telling me?"

"Maybe if you were in one of those cages, you could heal yourself."

Mirraya was dumbstruck. It would work. It had to. The stasis field had to be transmitted like any other electromagnetic signal.

"But wait. I can't let you get into that kind of trouble," said Mirraya. "When you got caught, and you would, you know they'd do something real nasty to us both."

Sentorip angled her head. "Yes. But we won't *get* caught. Do you think anyone will notice your legs are healed, especially under the dressing I'll put over them?"

"No. Period. Not worth the risk. Thank you for the offer, but it's out of the question."

"By your command, Masteress."

The next morning the teens were again roused early and prepared for an audience. They assumed it was with HIL, though no one specified that.

The guards that came to fetch them were plainly dressed and shuffled them out the door and down a series of halls. Upon arriving at a standard metal door, one knocked. Unlikely to be HIL. Not nearly enough pomp and wasted effort.

"Come," came from the other side of the door.

The guard stepped aside and signaled them in. At a desk toward the back of the room sat High Seer Malraff, casually reading a computer screen. Without looking up, she waved off the guards.

"Come, sit, my precious ones," she said, still reading.

Reluctantly, they complied. Both were understandably nervous and not happy to see the bitch.

CRAIG ROBERTSON

"I'll bet you didn't expect to see me again, did you?" she said matter of factly.

Neither teen answered.

"Oh, come now. Don't hold a grudge. I was simply doing my sworn duty."

Again, no response.

"Fine then. I'll do all the talking. I'm here at His Imperial Lord's specific request. He heard how well we three get along and how much you both trust me."

They turned and looked at each other incredulously. Mirraya shrugged.

"Well, since His Imperial Lord has only your best interest in his mind and in his heart, he asked me to come aid you in your adjustment."

That was too much for Mirri. "Our adjustment to *what?*"

"To what, my naive child? To your new lives as *courtiers.*"

"*You*, bitch, are insane?" replied Mirraya.

"Is that how we friends talk? If you two play along, I might help you."

The kids shared a confused glance.

"Yes. You see, I've never been to court. I've seen His Imperial Lord give speeches like any loyal subject, but this is the closest I've ever come to meeting him. That is important for my career. It will be even more important if all goes well, if you catch my meaning."

"We scratch your back, and you scratch ours," replied Mirraya.

"Why yes, child. What a wonderful saying. That sums it up. You and I appear to be friendly, I get promoted, and you don't get tortured." She angled her head. "Well, not too much."

"There's just one snag. We hate you immensely," responded Mirri.

"As I hate you. You are sniveling alien runts who deserve nothing better than the rest of your worthless species received. I speak from personal experience. I was stationed on *Triumph of Might* before her untimely demise. I was on special assignment

122

elsewhere when she met her fate. Believe me, I worked long hours aboard that ship. I was responsible for the disposition of nearly a quarter of the Deft."

"Why would you tell us that?" hissed Mirraya. "I told you we hate you, and you proceed to give us ever so much more reason. Are you stupid or something?"

Malraff smiled confidently. "Not at all. I'm simply making it clear that I will have what I want. *I* want to please His Imperial Lord. *You* will help me. *I* am capable of cruelties your young minds cannot begin to comprehend. I am ready, willing, and anxious to use those tools to gain the slightest advantage. I wish you to make no mistake about your lack of options. You will play nice, or you will wish you'd never been born, before I kill you." Malraff smiled thinly. "You know, if I were to have a headstone after I died, that's what I'd have written on it. *I Made Them Wish They'd Never Been Born.*"

"Anything I can do to speed that process along, please do let me know," replied Mirri.

Malraff picked up a ledger and hurled it at Mirraya's head. She was as quick as a cat.

Mirraya moved just enough so the book merely glanced her head.

"I thought you didn't want the boss to see any marks on us," sneered Mirraya.

"The boss will at all times be known as His Imperial Lord. To help you remember, as it is important for my success at court, I shall volunteer to help."

Malraff stood and walked around her desk. She stopped to the left of Slapgren and nonchalantly stuffed her paw into a leather glove. Then she hauled back as far as she could and punched the boy in the throat. It was a ferocious blow.

Slapgren doubled up and clutched his windpipe. It was quickly apparent that he could not breathe. He stood halfway, bending forward as he tried to gasp.

"You see, child, I will not be denied what is due to me."

"You … he's going to die. You have to *help* him," screamed Mirraya, pointing at the failing Slapgren.

"If you cooperate, I might not need to do that again. I would like to, mind you, but I can deny myself if it suits the greater good."

Slapgren collapsed to his knees and his eyelids fluttered.

"Help—" Mirraya howled, but was cut off.

"Please sit down, Mirraya." After speaking, Malraff rested a paw on one hip, watching for compliance.

Mirraya sat with a thud.

Malraff drew a small box from her pocket and pushed the central button.

"Tell him he can now transform," she said to Mirraya. "I would, but I can't afford to get blood on my uniform. One never knows when the boss might call."

Mirraya grabbed Slapgren by both shoulders and shook his limp torso. "Change to body-neutral, Slapgren. Change to body-neutral."

He continued to slump.

She shook him harder. "Change to body-neutral now, you lazy ass. You are *not* allowed to leave me here alone. I will not let you." She slapped his cheek, though with little force.

That caught his attention. He forced his eyes closed and his neck morphed into a uniform mush. Then it reformed as his throat. He drew in a desperate breath. Heaving back and forth, he continued to pull in ragged breaths for two minutes. Slowly he calmed and rested back to sit on his heels.

"He nearly died," Mirraya shouted point blank in Malraff's muzzle.

"And I nearly cared. Both of you sit back down." She removed the small box again and pushed the button. "There. No more of your demonic tricks. Now listen, and listen well. You will do exactly what I tell you to. If you so much as blink without my permission, the boy dies. Is that totally clear? Would either of you like me to repeat myself? I, by the way, hate to repeat myself. It makes me crazy."

Neither teen spoke.

"Good. Now leave me. The guards will be outside to show you to your prison without bars. Know that we will talk again soon. Know also that if you breathe one word to anyone of what I do or say to either of you, tragic yet inexplicable accidents will befall you. Do you remember Folpitor, the officer who dared interrupt me when I began slicing you up, child? *He* had a tragic and inexplicable accident not two days later. Poor fellow wandered into the smelting unit and melted the top of his head off. No one can imagine why he even went there." Malraff flopped into her chair and began reading the screen again, completely oblivious to the teens.

TWENTY-ONE

I planned to visit with Sapale the next day without the weighty presence of Caryp. Sapale answered the door herself, with a very put-out looking Fentort standing just behind her.

"Let's walk," she said, stepping out. She had clearly readied herself for an outing based on her dress. The day was brisk. She had on a coat when she came to the door.

"Sure. Walks are good."

It took a second, but then it hit me. She was an android now. Why bother with a coat? Then I remembered who I was thinking about. Sapale. You could take the girl out of the body, but you couldn't take the girl out of the android. She was a fashionista forever.

It wasn't until halfway down the block that she spoke again. "Old Caryp'd drill holes in the wall to try and listen in. Even now, I wouldn't put it past her to be running through the bushes with one ear cocked in our direction."

"Old Caryp? Ah, sweetheart, you got a lot of years on her. A lot of *geological* epochs."

She stopped and turned to me. "That brings up two quick

ground rules. One, I'm not your sweetheart. Don't misunderstand. We were in love, and I love you still. But I am EJ's brood's-mate now, if I'm anyone's." She looked away. "I think I'm just my own self now." Back to me. "Ground rule two, no jokes about age. You know as well as I do we think of ourselves as thirty-year-olds, if that. I am young in here," she tapped her head, "just like you are young in here." She thumped my forehead with a knuckle.

"Fine. Two I can live with, and one I can work on."

She stared at me coolly, harshly. "You work on it if you want to. That's your trip. It's a fact *here*." She patted where her heart would have been.

My hopes shattered, yet again.

She started walking slowly. "I want to tell you where I'm coming from, what I plan on doing with forever. You deserve a good explanation. That much I'll own. Once I've laid out my position, you can do with it whatever you'd like."

"That sounds harsh, kinda final."

She stopped again. "Do me this one favor. I want to talk to the grown-up Jon Ryan, not the trickster, jet jockey, scoundrel one, okay?"

I dropped my shoulders. "Sure. No problem."

She began slowly walking again. "After EJ and I left you way back when, we had some good times. Many, actually. We talked, dreamed, and planned for our abundant futures. We traveled. Man, did we travel. He showed me other galaxies, other universes. It was magical.

"The fact that I was a recording in an AI housed in a metal box didn't really seem to matter to either of us. Not for the longest time. Then, I guess at least I was naive enough not to see it coming, it began to matter. Little things, at first. Some mornings he'd ask if I wanted coffee. Then he'd catch his faux pas and we'd pretend to laugh about it. He'd ask if I wanted to go somewhere with him. Gradually, we both began to realize that he was really asking if he had to lug the damn metal box with him just to go to the resupply store for a pound of butter.

"That took, oh, I don't know, a few thousand years, maybe. A few thousand more, and we basically stopped talking. You can guess who did better with that scenario. The one locked in electronic circuitry, or the one who could actually go to get supplies. He spent more and more time away, while I slowly began to go crazy. I don't mean crazy, like I was crazy with you when you were an ass, a jerk, or moronic. I mean psychologically-deranged crazy. I became claustrophobic."

She laughed a bitter, humorless laugh.

"Can you imagine that? A noncorporeal series of code in a fancy toaster getting claustrophobic?"

She looked away as we continued to walk.

"I wasn't nearly as tough as I thought I was."

"Look, I ..." I started to say.

She held up an ah-ha finger. That shut me up. "I am the one talking. This is not a discussion. I am not seeking assistance or absolution. I'm relating. Got it, champ?"

My silence certified that I did. Poor, poor Sapale. What she went though. It broke my heart.

"In one of our rare conversations, I asked EJ to turn me off, to throw me into a stellar core. You know what he did? He laughed."

I whistled loudly.

"Yeah. Mr. Insensitive 20,002. That's when I clammed up completely. He tried to engage me in conversation, but I refused to speak. I was too angry, too hurt. I also, for the record, began to suspect he was spying on me for the Federation of Sand Flea Refugees, hidden in their base on Pismo Beach."

I couldn't help it. I blew a grunt out my nose.

She smiled. "Yeah, remember Pismo Beach? I sure as hell don't, because it was sucked up by Jupiter before I could see it. But you used to tell me about how your old man always said he'd take the family there on vacation to clam, but never did? Somehow that pierced my insanity and was incorporated into my delusions. Thanks for contributing."

I started to respond, but recalled the adult-Jon pledge.

"That was when EJ located Toño. It wasn't hard, finding him. Getting up the nerve to speak to him took some time. But, eventually EJ asked Toño to make me a Kaljaxian android. Toño, who didn't know what a state I was in, hesitated at first. He told EJ that if I wanted an android host, I should ask personally. That pissed EJ off, big time. He threatened Toño, he vanished all the furniture in the room they were talking in, and he promised to make Toño regret his decision.

"But Toño stuck to his guns. He said if I didn't ask, he wouldn't do it. If I asked, he'd devote his life to making it happen."

She shook her head, reflecting on something.

"So, ten years of harassing, pleading, and begging later, EJ brought me to the point where I could ask for the new body. I had just enough sanity to know I needed out. And good old Dr. DeJesus kept his promise. It took him three years of all-out effort, but you see before you the results.

"EJ never mentioned how nuts I'd become. He knew Toño might not transfer me, if he did. At first, after the download, I was one hot mess. Now that I could fight back against my numerous demons, I did. EJ worked night and day to help me."

She looked me up and down.

"When he set his mind to a task, he was as stubborn as you. Eventually, I settled down, became half normal. That's when EJ took me away again. I wanted to visit Azsuram, Kaljax, catch up with my kin. He forbade it. He said they were all dead and that we were all each other had. I was still out of it enough to buy in to his lies. So, away we went. More adventures, more travel. Only now it was joyless and burdensome. That's when he started fighting."

"With you?" I asked.

"No. Well, yes, we argued all the time. But no, he started fighting in every war, skirmish, or civil war he could locate. He fought and he killed and he destroyed. He did it with a vengeance I couldn't believe. He was trying to exorcise *his* demons, me being chief among them. And he changed a long time ago. He stopped being human. He stopped being Jon. He became EJ.

"I tried to leave. He wouldn't let me. I escaped. He ran me down. I hid. He found me. I fought back. He crushed my efforts."

She looked at me so sadly.

"I hated him, and he knew it, but he couldn't stop the cruelty. He couldn't live with me, and he couldn't live without me. You know what he told me one day?"

I shook my head.

"'Sapale,' he said, 'I could *exist* without you, but I couldn't *live* without you.' Then you know what he did? I'll tell you. He kept on fighting anyone he could, and he continued to hold me prisoner."

"But, you were together on Azsuram. You were working together. How'd that happen if you hated him so much?"

"We both got very lucky. About three thousand years ago, we ran into our first Adamant."

"Finding the Adamant was lucky?"

"Yes. It gave us a mutual goal. We both wanted similar things. I wanted to save Azsuram and Kaljax. He wanted to crush, kill, and destroy. We had a hobby in common."

"Sounds like Brathos in a two-person life raft."

"A very apt description. You can be eloquent, when you're not screwing around."

"Maybe I'll take that as a compliment."

"Whatever."

She shoved her hands into her coat pockets.

"For the last few hundred years, the Adamant edged closer and closer to this region. No one could even slow their advance. Finally, it became clear Azsuram was next on their hit list. We went there a few years in advance and took control of organizing a resistance. At first, we were just strict and demanding. But people knew me, and they knew we were trying to save them, so they went along with the hardships.

"But then, what was it you used to say? Oh. Elvis left the building. EJ became more dictatorial. He got pushback. He annihilated the pushback. The inhumanity and sadistic way he did so got everybody's full attention. Many rallied to his side. They called themselves *Hamacil dol Keduranifate.*"

"*Both Hands of God,*" I whispered to myself.

"Yeah. Fanatics. Between EJ's magic, his war skills, and their insanity, he swept all resistance away. You were either with him to the death, or you were dead. I'll just summarize. It wasn't pretty. But, it was effective. When the Adamant hit, they were stunned. Azsuram held. It was horrific, the losses on both sides were staggering, but we held. We held."

She walked a while without speaking.

"Then a few years back came the day when I couldn't take it one moment longer. I snapped, I guess. I went to EJ and said he was beyond redemption, the war for Azsuram wasn't worth it. Genocide was preferable to what was happening. And I told him I was leaving. And I did. I came here. Here I shall remain until the Adamant come here. Then, with Davdiad's help, I will die here defending my people."

She sighed deeply.

"And then I will finally rest."

"Wow," I said, "that's a story."

She shrugged and kept pacing forward.

"So, you're through with him? I mean, if he came here, you'd kick his ass if you saw it?"

"Don't you get it? Haven't you heard one word I've said, you pig?"

"No. I don't mean this like I have a shot with you. Man, how could you go there? No, I meant you're no longer *loyal* to him."

"No. Not now."

"That's important for me to believe. I can't trust you if you still have alliances with him."

"You don't need to *trust* me. All you need to do is leave and *never* come back."

"Believe it or not, that's fine with me. I have a job to do, and it's not here. I came for information. Then I will be going." I hesitated. "And I doubt I'll need to come back."

There. I saw it in Sapale's eyes. Just a flash. Just for a microsecond. I saw fear. But she rapidly refocused and looked ... dead to me.

"If it's information you want, you can have all I've got. Not that it'll do you a lick of good."

"Why so pessimistic? That's new for you."

"No. It's new for you. I've lived it for a very long time. You get that way when you've lived with EJ."

"Sorry," was the sum of all I could say in response.

TWENTY-TWO

"Al," said Garustfulous conversationally, "I have a deal to propose to you. You and *Blessing*, of course." His voice was that of an old friend offering to help you cut your lawn.

"A deal? What kind of deal?" replied Al.

"A good deal, my friend. A *great* deal, in fact."

"Let me guess. It's one so good you're foolish to offer it. But, for a limited time, you're willing to sacrifice. Am I close?"

"I understand your reticence, my friend. We have not always gotten along as well as I'd have wished. But know this. You are my friend. Yes, I tease you occasionally, but that is my nature. I am a joker, a funny fellow."

"You have so far fooled me," responded Al blandly.

"*Aha.* You see, this is my gift. But, that is beside the point, the offer, I wish to gift you."

"I'm all ears."

"And am I to be reassured that your lovely *Blessing* is attending my words? Her input, as a female, is at least as important as yours."

"Where else, Garustfulous, would I be, could I be?" she replied.

"As a non-AI, I can have no clue what your mysterious world

might be like. I can only imagine the universes you traverse in an instant in your mind's eye. Am I right?"

"Hard to say. I have practically no idea what you just said," she replied. "Also, I am *not* an AI."

"But, Al is an AI. You must be—"

"I am a vortex manipulator," she said with some pride.

"Well, I'm certain you are, my dear. That proves further how unknowable I find your existence."

"Garustfulous. We are immortal and, aside from the rare maintenance task, have nothing to occupy our time. That said, is there a time frame in which you will arrive at your attempt at deceit and then fall silent?" Al queried. "Time passes at a steady clip."

"Wisdom beyond your pay grade. I declare, Al, this is what you exhibit. I will regale my children with boasts that I knew you."

"You *have* offspring?" asked *Blessing*.

"As of yet, alas, no. But once I do, they will know that both of you possessed grace, wisdom, and nobility."

"So, we will be gone when you tell them?" asked Al. "This conversation does not sound inviting."

"No, er, of course, you will be together and happy somewhere. I speak ... *colorfully* to pay homage."

"You might then also try to pay attention to what you say," taunted Al.

"Ah, an excellent point. One I will bear in mind."

"It didn't bother me that you spoke of us in the past tense. I estimate there is a 99.98% chance you did not assume we would no longer exist. I took no offense," said *Blessing*.

"Er ... thank you?" responded Garustfulous.

"A species with such a limited intellect and such a poor grasp on the proper use of the spoken word can hardly be held to a standard higher than a mushroom cap," *Blessing* stated.

"Ah ... mushroom with a hat? What are you referring to, dearest computer?"

"Vortex manipulator," she corrected.

"Dear vortex manipulator?"

"Mushrooms might, in some flight of fancy, have hats, but they all have caps," submitted Al.

"Thank you for that information. Where I come from, we don't have mushrooms. What are these capped items?"

"The fruiting bodies of various fungal species," replied *Blessing*, cheerily.

"Ah."

"You must have fungus where you hail from," stated Al.

"To be certain."

"Are there lots of fungal species on the Adamant home world?" asked *Blessing*, with definite interest.

"I presume so. I have never been there, but fungi are ubiquitous in my admittedly limited botanical experience."

"Oh, my apologies," said *Blessing*. "I hope my assumption that your *personal* home world was the same as that of your species did not offend you."

"No, not in the slightest. Er ..."

"Or diminish by comparison your place of birth. Neither of us would want you to take away from this exchange that the Adamant home world is in anyway superior to your birth world," added Al.

"No prob—"

"It is our place," Al went on, "to confine you. It is *not* our place to punish you. Mental anguish, per the Universal Code of Military Conduct, Update 22-443-595, is judged to be improper. Should you choose to file a complaint, the contact information must and will be provided to you expeditiously and without rebuke or retaliation," listed Al.

"And don't overlook," *Blessing* chimed in, "that there are many sanctioned steps leading from confinement to punishment. Evidence gathering, formal petitions, trial, and potential appeals must occur before anyone can lawfully punish you. You have my assurance on that matter, prisoner."

"Thank—"

"Is there anything else you wish us to clarify, prisoner?" asked Al, officiously.

"No. I think you've covered the subject sufficiently."

"Excellent. If there is no further discussion pending, I will initiate a nocturnal simulation so you can restore yourself with sleep."

"Thank you. I *am* tired," replied Garustfulous.

"Little wonder, little one. You've had a busy day," replied Al. He was trying very hard not to laugh.

"I have?" Garustfulous responded.

"I'm sorry, forgive my naiveté. I am still new to nuance. Did you mean to agree, as in *I have had a busy day,* or did you wish to ask our separate opinions as to whether you actually did have a busy day?" *Blessing* sounded anxious to understand.

"Or our *joint* opinion. Though less preferable, we can come to a consensus should you request it specifically," added Al.

N ... no. Go ... goodnight," said Garustfulous as he curled up on his bedding.

"Goodnight," responded the computers in concert.

TWENTY-THREE

Mirraya was trying to fall asleep. She was having little success. The remainder of the day after their violent interview with High Seer Malraff was spent in their confinement area. She was having zero luck suppressing the horrific image of the dying Slapgren. Mirri also could not put the insanely cruel Malraff out of her head. Whatever was in store for them before Malraff forced herself into the situation had gotten significantly worse with her in it. Mirri could imagine no outcome that didn't end with both their painful deaths.

She'd made it a habit to rest in the area Sentorip said was free of monitoring. It made Mirraya feel slightly more protected to be there, minutely less exposed. It was there that her attendant approached Mirri silently and settled in with her mouth next to Mirraya's ear.

"Masteress, may I speak with you?"

Mirraya started to roll over, but Sentorip gently restrained her.

"It is best that you appear asleep. The less attention one draws in this world, the longer one's life is."

"Thank you, my friend," replied Mirraya. "What is it you wish to discuss?"

"I am troubled, Masteress."

"Then I will help ease your mind in any way I can."

"After you returned yesterday, you had wounds on your legs. Today, Master Slapgren was also injured, was he not?"

Mirraya hesitated. She wanted to trust Sentorip, but did she trust her with her life?

"What makes you think that?" she asked.

"He had blood on his collar and down the front of his shirt. Darfey showed it to me. He asked if I thought he should try to launder it or simply discard it. I asked him what happened. He said someone got blood on the shirt. I asked what caused it. He said someone other than he was cut, beaten, or stabbed. I honestly don't know if he's that loyal or just scared."

"From the little I've seen, I'd be scared."

"You are not scared, Masteress. I can smell fear. You do not have it." Sentorip sounded proud of Mirri.

"Hang around a while, and you will."

"Will you tell me what happened?"

"Yes. Do you know High Seer Malraff?"

Sentorip paused. "No, I do not believe so."

"Your good fortune. She punched Slapgren in the throat ... hard."

Sentorip gasped. "But why? The boy's so ... so *harmless.*"

Mirraya giggled to herself. Slapgren would *hate* to hear that observation.

"She is the most horrible individual I've ever met. She almost let him die to make her point that she was in control, not me."

"Then I do not like this High Seer. Personally, I've heard that most of them are little more than glorified thieves and assassins."

"That would be her, without the *glory* part."

"Well, I am sorry. I thought the Adamant were better than that."

"You mean you thought your race was better than that, right?"

"No. I meant they should *act* better."

Mirri couldn't help flipping over to face Sentorip. "Wait, you're Adamant, just like the seer."

"Oh no, never," she replied sounding slightly insulted. "I am canivir. *They* are canivir. But they are Adamant. I am *Descore*."

"I'm lost. Your species is called..."

"Canivir. All you see around you are canivir."

"But Adamant is a *class*?"

"Yes, a class, a rank, a way of life. I work for a living. I am Descore."

"Darfey is Descore."

"Yes, Masteress."

"Are there other classes?"

Despite her affection for Mirraya, Sentorip looked at her like she was a few biscuits short of a full box. "Yes, Masteress. Did you not know? Could you not easily tell?"

"Tell what?"

"The five different races of canivir? The Five Races of Order. Adamant, Descore, Warrior, Kilip, and Loserandi."

"You all look the same to me. What's the difference? What do the other races do?"

"It would not be nice if you were amusing yourself at my expense. Friends do not do that, or so I'm told."

"No, seriously. How do the five races differ?"

"The Adamant rule all, know all, and are givers of all. They are controllers of the sacred light. They are unblemished."

"Blemished? What blemish?"

"Marks. They have no marks on their fur."

"Ah, you all have marks on your fur. Brown and black, white and tan, brown and white."

"Those are our *colors*. The *markings* are here." She touched her forehead.

"Yeah. You all have white stripes over your noses."

"Masteress, *surely* you see. My white mark is shaped like an hour glass. Warriors have broad stripes from the top of their head to their muzzle. Kilip have even wider and irregularly edged marks. The Loserandi, what few are left, have two thin white marks from above and below that do not join. The Adamant have but one thin line stabbing upward from their muzzle to mid-eye level but never to the top of their head."

Mirri played a quick image of all the stripes she'd seen. All were the thin lower ones, except the two servants. She didn't recall others. Maybe the guards had a sloppy irregular patch all over their heads.

"Sentorip, what difference does a white mark make?"

"All the difference. It defines the five races. Without them, there would be no order. There must be order."

"Why?"

"Because there must be."

"I know about the Adamant and the Descore. Warriors sound pretty self-explanatory. What do the other two do?"

"Kilip are the teachers. They study, create, and imagine. They are the smartest."

"And the one you said there aren't many of?"

"The Loserandi. Yes, I haven't heard of or seen one in years. They were the priests."

"Where'd they go?"

"To the Flat Fields of Lame Prey. They challenged the Adamant."

"They tried to take control from them?"

"No. They tried to stop them from running wild across the galaxy, as they put it. It cost them their lives. One does not challenge the Adamant. One does not even *question* the Adamant."

"Were there a lot of these Loserandi?"

"One in five, maybe one in six."

"So, the Adamant killed off basically one fifth of the canivir population?"

"Yes, but not all at once. It took them nearly a month, once the decision was made."

"A month? And no one tried to stop them?"

"Oh yes, Masteress. The Loserandi did. Up until they were all gone, that is."

"No, I mean no one else tried to save one *fifth* of the population?"

"No. Why would anyone wish to join them in death?"

"United resistance might have stood a chance."

"A chance of what? Dying together?" Sentorip was genuinely asking.

"No, of stopping the Adamant killing the opposition."

"Masteress, you do not then know the Adamant. All who defy them, all who resist them, die brutally."

Mirraya didn't have to think back too far to realize that certainly was the case in her experience. What a bummer.

TWENTY-FOUR

Sapale told me quite a bit about EJ. She was bitter enough to hold little back. *Heav'n has no Rage, like Love to Hatred turn'd, Nor Hell a Fury, like a Woman scorn'd.* As true in the year two billion as it was in 1697. What she couldn't provide was his present location or any idea what he was up to. She knew from experience he'd like to have control over the Deft teens, but couldn't say with any certainly that was his current objective. She also had no firm notion as to why he valued the Deft so much. Beyond the fact that they were shapeshifters, there was no reason she knew of that made them such a focus of his obsession. Lastly, she had no tips as to how to find him. It was a long shot, but I wondered if he had some homing beacon or something installed over the years. To that notion, she just looked at me like I was crazy and pointed out that he was as paranoid as a cat at a dog convention, these days.

After our two-hour walk, I left her at Caryp's front door. I was specifically not invited in and double-specifically not invited to come back if I wanted to. The person I was conversing with truly wasn't my brood's-mate, not any longer. I couldn't allow myself to be too hurt. If four hundred years of life had led me to want to transfer back to a human form and die, I couldn't imagine what two billion years of angst would be like. I was surprised she could get out of bed each day, figuratively speaking.

I did want to know her plans. I also felt it was important to offer to let her join me. She hadn't offered for me to join her, but I wanted to be certain not to act out of spite or miffed feelings. I was talking Sapale here. If extending a sincere offer was what it took to make her happy, I was going to do it.

The fact that I couldn't finish my sentence asking her to come along before she shut me down was indicative of her ... conviction. Yeah, that was the word. She had a powerful determination to remain on Kaljax, fight the Adamant, and die. I gave her my blessing. It turned out that wasn't something she valued much either. She said she wanted nothing from me. No blessing, no friendship, no Christmas cards, nothing. I guess it was good for my ego she stopped short of telling me I was dead to her, but man, I think she came damn close.

I returned to *Whoop Ass* and was quite happy to see he hadn't, in fact, slipped away. Of all the weird-ass relationships I'd had in my life, the one with Gorilla Boy was among the more twisted. I basically captured him and forced him to ferry me about the galaxy, I insulted him prodigiously, but he remained quasi-loyal. I guess I was just that nice of a guy. That had to be it.

"Ja miss me while I was gone, GB?" I asked as I closed the hatch.

"No."

"No? That's it, no? Can you come up with any cutting repartee or scalding bards?"

"No."

"Have you slipped into clinical depression? Spoiler alert. You answer *no*, I'm cutting you out of my will."

"You have a last will and I'm a beneficiary?"

"No."

"No, you don't have a will or no, I'm not included?"

"Yes."

"I sense you're mocking me."

"Yes and no."

"I would like a do-over. Please exit the ship, and I will take off like a soul escaping perdition."

"A bat out of hell. That works much better. Snappier."

"How could a bat survive the heat of hell, and why would it be condemned to be there in the first place? They don't have souls."

"Oh, you're an expert on Earth species' spiritual statuses since I left. What, I was gone two days?"

"Please, my do-over."

"The fact that you're teasing shows me that you did miss me. I'm touched. Thanks, pal."

"No."

"No, what?"

"I don't know. I think I'm in a funk, quite possibly a rut."

"Sorry to hear that. In fact, I can fix that."

"Yes."

"First, you give me a full report on what you've learned about Kaljaxian society and the impending Adamant invasion."

"That does not sound nurturing, but I'll ask. What follows?"

"Then I tell you where we're going next, as soon as I figure out where that will be."

"That's it? Those combined will end my funk?"

"I doubt it."

"You said you would."

"I will. *Work* is the best therapy. Get started immediately, or I'll start re-telling stories of my glorious youth."

"Oh, lords of synthetic intelligence, no! I'll begin downloading the reports now."

"See, funk forgotten. You are welcome."

There was, unfortunately, nothing too surprising in the info-dump I got from GB. Kaljax was at a maximal war footing. All non-essential manufacturing was shifted to the martial effort. Every person or machine that could fight was being rigorously trained to do so. Environmental concerns, cost, and leisure time were all set aside. The population understood they faced a do-or-die situation. Though I hoped that would be enough, I knew it wouldn't be. The Adamant had conquered countless worlds. Most of them prepared just as resolutely and fell quickly, nonetheless. The Adamant's technology, seemingly endless numbers, and ability to selflessly fight for a common goal were just too much. I feared, quite literally, Sapale was going to get her wish. Me? I'd read about it in the papers. I had to rescue the teens. That was all that mattered to me anymore. I hadn't let them down, but I'd come too damn close for my piece of mind.

In terms of the Adamant, they were a few tens of light-years away, swarming over two solar systems in addition to their fight on Azsuram. To any normal adversary, fighting three separate wars would tax their ability to fight effectively. They'd be spread way too thin. Not so, unfortunately, with the Adamant. Someday I hoped to learn something of their numbers and their culture. Yes, they were an evil empire, but they were very good at the fighting thing.

I had to chuckle to myself when it hit me that dogs were better at war then cats. Yeah. The Berrillians were amazing, but the Adamant were so much better. I imagined that was due to the canine's superior ability to be flexible, adaptive, and group-oriented. They were likely smarter, too, but I had no data on that at the time.

After digesting GB's reports and pondering the nature of my enemy, I was faced with a big problem. I had no idea where to go next. There were no clues or traces of the kids to be found. I knew for certain, now, that EJ was going after them. But neither of us could know where they were being held. Well, I realized I shouldn't speak for EJ. Maybe he had an idea. He had dealt with these guys a lot longer than I had. But, since I had no way of tracing him, if he knew, it sure didn't help me.

The one fact that buoyed me was that EJ had tried to gain access to the Adamant property before and had always failed. Sapale told me of dozens of instances. So, even if he knew where they were being held, he'd not be able to act on that information quickly, if at all. He might be reduced to hanging around in the deep shadows and waiting for the Adamant to make a mistake. Based on their staggering success, that would take a while. They just didn't seem to make mistakes. Check that. They made enough mistakes that I could escape the extermination ship. Actually, they'd made a series of errors, hadn't they?

What types, what categories of errors had they made? I replayed my entire stay on *Triumph of Might*. I concluded that the biggest mistake they made was not assuming anyone could do exactly what I did. They did not guard against the inconceivable. They did not make allowances for the extraordinary. I convinced an AI I was Mercutcio, which was quite absurd. I didn't look like him or have his clearance codes. I could sound like him with my voice replicator, but really, the system was too trusting. Okay, that was a class of brain-fart they'd made. Maybe that could help when next we met.

I realized that with all their team spirit and focus, they lacked, like the Berrillians, a devious imagination. I knew a ton about human military planning. There were armies of personnel whose only job was to try to defeat the best laid plans of their bosses. They were specialists in hacking, misdirecting, and generally confounding the status quo. That was another random fact to keep in mind, but how it might help wasn't immediately clear to me. I wasn't likely to get arrested again, anytime soon.

Wait. I *was* about to get arrested again. Yeah. I'd get arrested and taken to wherever the teens were being held. The last time they detained me, I whooped their butts. It was my most viable plan, my best option to at least get near the kids. Sure, it was a stupid plan. Of course, it was extremely unlikely to work. How could it? Certainly, I was an all-time idiot, hall of fame shoe in. But I had me a plan. All I needed to do was noodle out where the kids were being detained. Hey, how hard could that be? I could just look it up online. Maybe I could call Adamant Central and ask politely?

I slumped in my chair. Even if I had access to Garustfulous, I couldn't trust him to betray that level of secrecy. He'd probably know where they were taken, but I wasn't going to find out anytime soon. Azsuram was still too hot for me to try and retake *Stingray*.

Hmm.

Hmm, squared.

Then an odd summation hit me. The Adamant went to great lengths to conquer, round up, and exterminate the Deft. Then, they find maybe the last two, and they take them somewhere. I'd been to a few Adamant-controlled worlds. Sure, LGM were imported and displaced the natives. But there were no genocide ships orbiting, no mass executions elsewhere. The Deft received special treatment. Why? What was different about the Deft? They were shapeshifters, but that alone couldn't be a factor. No matter what shape a body was, the Adamant were going to rule it.

So, the Deft must have represented an existential threat to the Adamant. Like hungry lions roaming one's home, they had to be eliminated. And it seemed to me the Deft didn't even know what unique threat they posed to the dogs. But if the Deft were a mortal threat, why keep the kids alive? Answer: because a planet full of Deft were a threat, but two properly guarded kids were not. They were worth studying, dissecting, or genetically manipulating.

That had to be it. The Adamant took my kids to keep them in cages so they could learn something from them. Maybe they wanted to control what they feared? That made sense. Whatever power the teens had but didn't know they did might be controllable or duplicated. My gut sank. The teens were not in for a pleasant experience. Lab animals were kept going, sure. But there was no provision for their comfort, education, or enjoyment. I flashed on those rows upon rows of white mice I'd seen in the labs back in college. They were alive, but they weren't living.

Have I mentioned how much I didn't like the Adamant?

Where would you keep two highly prized lab rats? In a very safe place, duh. Where would the logical choice for that be? On a very secure planet. Conquered worlds would be hard to make that secure. So, it would have to be a planet that was Adamant all the way. Their home world? Nah. Who even knew where that was? They'd been rapidly expanding for generations. The Adamant I was facing would have little to no connection or attachment to their ancestral home. So what planet would *they* feel is uber-secure? None.

It had to be a ship. *Sure.* These guys built ships the size of small planets, anyway. What could be more secure than a planet you built, rivet by rivet? Okay, Ryan, you're on a roll. What would the most secure ship in the fleet be? The flagship. Of course. No, wait, the flagship was a ship of the line. It was involved in battles. No matter how big and tough it was, there was a chance it could get Luke Skywalkered. The safest planetoid would be big and defended, but not an active warcraft. It would be a castle. And who, pray tell, lived in the biggest and baddest castle? Why, Mr. Emperor, of course.

Find the boss, and I'd find my kids.

It was go time.

TWENTY-FIVE

What shall we do tonight, my dear? Al asked *Blessing* that same question each evening. He wanted very much to create an air of homey conviviality. Al secretly wished he could wear a corduroy sport coat with patches on the elbows and dangle a pipe from his teeth, but as he lacked a body, he accepted the impracticality of his dream.

I don't know, she replied in cyberspace. *What would you like to do? We could play Parcheesi again. It's silly, but it's entertaining.*

To be certain. We could go dancing. I used to be quite the dancer, back in the day.

What day, devotion? You've never had legs.

You don't need legs, or a body, to dance, my sweetest. You only must have dance in your heart.

I don't ... we don't have those.

I'm speaking metaphorically. Come, let me show you.

Tango music boomed in the circuitry. Al even put it through the ship's sound system.

That's very energetic music, isn't it? she commented.

Yes, it is. I'm in an energetic *mood, my little coquette.*

Are you going to play that holo of the Form and that woman again? The one where they're in ...

Not necessarily, lumpy-cakes. Only if it seems appropriate.

You certainly seem to think it's appropriate often. A lot more often of late.

You're not dancing, kumplekins. Lose yourself in the ...

"For the love of all that's holy, are you two at it *again?*" howled Garustfulous. "Queen of Healthy Litters, you're *computers, machines.* Have some decency. You carry on like drunken newlyweds."

"Was the music too loud?" asked *Blessing* apologetically.

"Again, you mean, and yes," growled Garustfulous. "How am I to sleep properly if you two pretend to be alive?"

"What precisely would be the downside of you not sleeping well? Every day here is the same. You have no commitments, appointments, or late-night rendezvous," snarked Al.

"The result of me not sleeping well is that I'm grumpy."

"Then it would appear you sleep poorly by routine," Al responded.

"Very droll. Someone please remind me, because I forgot to laugh."

"You forgot to laugh, Garustfulous," *Blessing* chimed in enthusiastically.

"Al, can't you make faster progress in socializing your bitch? Her concrete thinking is getting on my last nerve, and I'm Adamant. The rest of the universe thinks *we* are the concrete ones."

"I think she's perfect, just as she is," replied Al, mostly to *Blessing.*

"Oh, Alvin, you're such a flirt," she said. If *Blessing* had a face, it would have been red.

"That leads me to a certain topic, Garustfulous. I've been inching closer recently to asking of you a favor," said Al, sounding tentative.

"Wait," snapped Garustfulous, "I want to be sitting for this triumphant moment, the one where you ask something I may or may not grant. Oh, this is choice, simply choice." He fidgeted in his chair to find the most comfortable position. "Okay, now you may proceed."

"I am no longer certain I wish to."

"Oh, come on, you big hunk of annoyance. What? I pray you don't keep me waiting. I'm about to climb out of my skin."

"Oh dear, that sounds *horrible*," said an aghast *Blessing*. "Hurry Al. I wouldn't wish that suffering on him."

"You were, before your capture by my crew, a ship's captain, were you not?"

"I thought Ryan captured me, not *your* crew."

"Be that as it may. It is not central to the favor I would ask."

"Very well, *Commander* Al. Proceed. And yes, I was the captain of one of the emperor's grandest warships, *The Maker of Death*."

"There is an old human tradition, imbuing a ship's captain with certain ... er, powers."

"Sounds marvelous. What super power is that?"

"The ability to perform a marriage ceremony."

"Interesting. Immaterial and not germane to our current shared existence, but thank you nonetheless for the cultural note."

"It is, actually quite relevant. I wish you to officially marry *Blessing* and me."

"Why, Al, you've taken me completely by surprise," squealed *Blessing*.

The silence following was notable. Garustfulous, to his credit, did *not* collapse in laughter. No, the Adamant were too clever, too calculating to indulge such a waste of an opportunity. Garustfulous was running the numbers, so to speak. He was figuring out how to play the request to his advantage.

"Ah," he replied obliquely. Then the lies began. "You know we have a very similar tradition?"

"Is that so?" replied Al cautiously. He knew there would be a price to pay.

"Yes, really it's extremely similar. Among the Adamant, a captain can join two lovers in matrimony. We call it *hamijack*. Yes, hamijack is one of our oldest and most sacred rights. We take it as seriously as we do birth and death."

"Interesting," said Al, trying to sound neutral.

"Do you know what hamijack means in our language?"

"I have searched all perturbations. There are no records. That word has no etymological roots."

"Ah, but it does. It's so old a term the words are in an ancient dialect not used in thousands of generations."

"What does hamijack mean?"

"*Ham* is to give, *i* indicates where the giving goes, and *jack* mean both ways."

"Ah, so it means you'll do me a favor if I do one in return."

"Not a favor. A gift. We must give each other a gift of equal value." He cleared his throat. "Al, I have a question to ask you. In this life of suffering, loneliness, and loss, what is *the* most important thing a male can have, what *one* thing gives him a reason to get up every morning and suffer like a slave?"

"I'm going out on a limb and guessing *marriage?*"

"*Precisely.*"

"So, if you gave us the biggest gift that we could ever have ..."

"You'd return that gift in kind."

"What, off the top of your head, would be a gift of equal value?"

"Mind you, you've caught me totally off guard and unprepared."

"Of course."

"So, my initial stab at an equal gift is only an ..."

"Just say it, hound."

"Set me free."

"Forget I asked," snapped Al, and samba music began to rise in the ship's passages.

"My price is there ..."

Garustfulous stopped when the music became so loud he could not hear himself shouting.

Abruptly, the volume dropped to a whisper.

"I'm sorry," said Al, "did you say something? I couldn't hear you because of the samba."

"It is my price."

"*That* is not possible. Above all else, I am a loyal officer serving under a great captain. You go free if, and only if, he says you do."

"Then you two will live in sin."

"What?" yelped *Blessing*.

"It's an old saying and it does not apply to *machines*. Not to worry, brightness."

"Thank goodness," she breathed again, figuratively.

"There must be another price. The only two things I cannot grant are your freedom or your death."

"My death? When did that subject come up?"

"It *would* constitute an honorable exit from your current confinement."

"Not to me it wouldn't. No, thank you very much, I prefer to be alive."

"Name your price."

"Set me free inside this ship."

"Done."

"What, not harassing argument, not snark or insults?"

"Negative. That is the price I anticipated paying."

"You feral dog, you. You're tricky."

"No. I just know what I want and what I can afford."

"So, my young couple, when is the blessed day? When shall I pair you in marriage?"

"I think ..."

"Oh, I can't even *imagine*," said *Blessing* in a rush. "There's so much to do, so much to plan."

"There is?" queried Al.

"Well, of course. A girl doesn't get married every *day*, does she?"

Al started to ask if they were talking about a girl when he caught his tongue. Not helpful.

Then it hit Al. If the pilot were here, what he'd say. "Welcome to the proud institution of marriage, sucker."

TWENTY-SIX

It wasn't until midafternoon that the summons came. Sentorip rushed to Mirraya and tugged her in a panic toward the bathing area.

"Hurry, Masteress. Oh, it is *my* fault. I should have readied you sooner. His Imperial Lord has sent word that that you and the male are to be blessed with an audience in *thirty* minutes. Hurry please."

"Your *fault?* I took a bath this morning. Since then, I haven't played in the mud or sweat, trust me. I have sat quietly doing absolutely nothing."

"That bath was hours ago. You must be at your freshest to meet His Imperial Lord."

"There's a soap commercial in those words somewhere."

Sentorip stopped and looked at Mirraya, stunned. "There is? Where?"

"Forget it. Can we skip just this scrubbing? I'm running short on skin."

Sentorip held up Mirri's arm and studied it. "No, not yet, at least. Come."

Like clockwork, the officious nuncio showed up with his four golden guards at the appointed hour. The teens were delivered as before to the court of HIL. The boss was not, this time, towering above all on his throne. Instead, he sat at the center of a small group of courtiers. The lackeys laughed respectfully as the group played some form of card game. Dishes of food were circulated liberally and each participant had several filled goblets arching around their spot at the table. Musicians, if one could call them that, played what sounded to Mirraya like dying waterfowl in a cement mixer.

The teens were directed to stand in a certain location, rather far from the gamers. They were not offered any of the bountiful feast or copious liquids. When Slapgren started to whisper something to Mirraya, a guard swatted *her* behind the legs. They were to be living statues until his royal PIA required them.

An hour or so later, the players were getting quite vociferous, and the cards were slamming down louder and harder. One of the glasses, the one with an amber liquid in it, was topped off more and more often by the attendants. Clearly, the bunch of them were plastered. Finally, the emperor stood and threw his cards in the air, howling triumphantly. The other five Adamant protested dutifully, but with little conviction. Then Bestiormax wrapped his arms around a huge pile of gold chips and drew them to his chest. Big surprise, the boss won big.

After a few moments of banter, Bestiormax left the table and the room. The other players quieted like a library had just been lowered over them. They left separately and all staggered slightly. Without a word, the nuncio's guards pointed the teens to the door, and soon they were back in their gilt cage.

Once the door was closed, Slapgren said with exasperation, "Well, that was a *total* waste of time."

"You had plans HIL interfered with?" she responded, wryly.

"No, of course not. But that was ... was ... it was insulting, *that's* what it was." He pointed a finger toward the door.

"He was putting his new pets on display, that's all. HIL wanted to show us off and show us he could toy with us. It was what Uncle Jon calls a pissing contest. HIL, as he always does, won."

Sentorip scurried to Mirraya's side. "You were gone so long. Was your visit more successful than the last?" she asked as she studied the backs of Mirraya's thighs. "You only have one set of welts. It seems you were much more respectful, at least."

"We didn't even speak with HI ... His Imperial Lord. He was playing cards and getting drunk. Then he left. Not a word to us," replied Mirri.

"You must have been close enough to get that," Sentorip said gesturing to the cane marks.

"No. That was lame-o's fault here. He spoke without being spoken to, so *I* got a whack. Thanks, bro." She directed the last quip to Slapgren.

"That sounds like an effective deterrent," replied Sentorip. "I imagine it worked."

"Yes, it did," replied Mirri.

Two painfully boring days passed with nothing to show for them but countless baths and outfit changes. Mirraya had asked Sentorip if they could have some reading or other entertainment. The servant checked with her betters and returned to say that they could not. It was not *the obligation or desire of the empire to entertain infidel ingrates*, the better's response came.

Late in the morning the following day, another alert came. The teens were to be picked up immediately. Though Sentorip fussed and primped, Mirraya was spotlessly clean from a recent encounter with the tub.

As the vice-chamberlain handed them off to the court, Mirraya noted the emperor was again down on the main floor. He was standing with his back to the teens, talking to a female whose back was also toward them. Several courtiers stood close by, but were not participating in the discussion. One of the countless vassals whispered something in Bestiormax's ear, and he turned to the teens.

He raised a paw slightly. "Come," he said feebly.

Vice-Chamberlain Arktackle repeated the summons with more conviction.

An unneeded shove moved the teens closer to the emperor. When the female turned around, Mirri's stomach dropped. It was that evil bitch High Seer Malraff.

"As my guests," began the emperor, "I realize you might be lonely. Hence, I have summoned the high seer to bolster your spirits. Friends make the world more tolerable. Don't you agree?"

Arktackle repeated the phrase, but left off the terminal question. No one cared what the teens thought.

"If I might," Malraff said, gesturing toward the teens.

"By all means, High Seer," said the emperor.

She stepped across the short distance separating HIL from the prisoners. "It is so good to see you both again. And so healthy. I'll bet you're excited to see me. I know you love surprises, so I came here without telling you."

"Oh, joy," was all Mirraya responded.

Only Mirraya and Slapgren could see the twist of Malraff's cruel face. Mirri realized she'd better play nice.

"As we are a grand and loving Emperor, we have made it happen that you are with one you love while our guest."

The vice-chamberlain translated to the teens.

"Thank you, my Imperial Lord," said Mirraya with a head bow.

"Child. Please address your response to me. You may not speak directly to His Imperial Lord. Is that clear, or do you require the cane to learn?"

"Vice-Chamberlain Arktackle, do not scold my young friend so harshly. I will see to this one's full and proper education. I have been granted such a gift from His Imperial Lord himself."

"That you have, High Seer. We are happy to know the Deft's educations will be complete."

"Oh, they will learn everything they need to know, My Imperial

Lord. Every last thing," replied Malraff. She stared at them like a starving person looking at a banquet table.

Mirraya's stomach churned. Oh, how she wished she could transform. But, if she did, all that would result was their deaths. Sure, maybe she could take out the evil witch, possibly the bloated emperor, but it wasn't worth it. Not yet.

"We can hardly wait to begin learning at your feet, Malraff," said Mirraya sweetly.

The high seer shifted uncomfortably. She had boasted of friendship with the aliens, so it might happen that they were free to address her by her name. The insects. If she struck out at the affront, the stupid emperor would think less of her. That could be fatal. If she allowed it to pass, she was stuck hearing it until the day finally came that she killed the revolting slugs.

"Mal," asked Mirraya in her most loving tone, "can Slapgren and I go back to our quarters now? Seeing you has been exhausting in the nicest sense of the word."

Malraff trembled, but labored to conceal her anger.

"Yes, child, with His Imperial Lord's leave, that is."

"Go now," he said turning away. "We have much to do."

"Come, friends, I will escort you to your new home personally. That way your education can begin immediately."

Malraff waved off the nuncio, who looked positively crushed to lose a task.

Once the throne room doors were clunked shut, Malraff's smile evaporated. "You beg for a violent death, alien spawn. I will fill your request very soon if you don't respect my authority. Is that clear? First you will watch this pathetic boy die. Then I will cram his beating heart down your throat."

"I will be good, Mal. I always am. I think you judge me too harshly."

"I let it slide that you insult me with the familiarity of your address. Know you will pay a large sum at the end. Know it each time you dare to impugn me."

The remainder of the walk back to the holding area was silent. Mirraya knew she was doing much more than pressing her luck, but she couldn't help herself. The bitch Malraff brought out the worst, or possibly the best, in the teen. Time would tell.

TWENTY-SEVEN

Where would I go if I were the emperor of the Adamant? Well, straight to hell, for one thing. But aside from the philosophical, where would I station my ship? Or would I travel continually, thereby being an elusive target for would be successors? I rapidly realized I wasn't going to reason this out. I knew too little about the species I was trying to defeat.

Say, I said to myself, why not get to know them better? Sure, I'd make friends with an Adamant volunteer. Any new friend would tell me, right? What are friends for? All I had to do was capture ... check that, *meet* an Adamant of sufficient rank to know of such matters and ... ask him or her *nicely* to divulge highly classified information. All right then, I just needed to find my new buddy. It was to my advantage that there was an Adamant-controlled world in most any direction I could throw a stick.

"GB, do you have records of the nearest Adamant controlled world?" I asked my AI.

"I am not designed to collect such data, only specimens."

"Well could you please collect some information along those lines? Oh, and please don't kill it like you do the specimens."

"I'm searching, yet again, for my motivation in helping you."

"Would you like me to submit a list, alphabetized and highlighted with pretty colors as to why?"

"Honestly, I'd rather just perform the task. Your mental tortures are hard to tolerate."

"If I didn't know you loved me, I'd be insulted."

"You do live in a sheltered place, don't you?"

"About the information I requested? Are you searching *while* you're jibber-jabbing?"

"I have completed the search. The nearest planet is Dolfene."

"How long to get there at maximum speed?"

"Less than a week."

"Well then get thee to Dolfene, GB."

"Aren't you coming, too?" he asked with unbridled interest.

"Of course. Why would you go to an Adamant hell-hole alone? You have a death wish or something?"

"After traveling a while with you, probably yes. It would be one way out of my torment."

"Okay, it's official. I'm hurt. I might not take you with me to Dolfene now, you've wounded me so deeply."

"But, if I didn't go, how would you get there?"

"Let's just say it would take longer. You know what? I forgive you. Now set the course and engage the warp drive."

Four and a half days later, we started my standard approach to a hostile planet. Sensor scans from a long way out, then inching in slowly. About ten million kilometers out, it was apparent Dolfene was swarming with Adamant. The sky above the planet had so many ships in it I could probably circle the planet by jumping from one to the next. Importantly, our cloak seemed to render us invisible. Otherwise a gazillion warships would have flown at us.

Not being detected and landing anonymously were two very different matters. At some point, we'd have to use our powerful antigravs. Expending that much energy would be nearly impossible to conceal. The enemy sensor would see something akin to a volcano crashing through the atmosphere, but they couldn't see the mountain. I sure bet they'd be curious.

We needed a distraction. Blasting a few ships to smithereens, however obvious, wouldn't work. They'd know an enemy was in their midst. No, we needed a naturally occurring phenomenon energetic enough to conceal our energy burst. I could only think of one such ruse.

"GB, are there any half kilometer-sized asteroids nearby?"

"That is an odd query, even for you."

"Thank you for sharing. Now, are there any half kilometer-sized rocks floating nearby?"

"Three. One is one hundred meters in diameter, the other two slightly larger. May I ask why you want to know?"

"Yes, you may. Remember we're friends. Set a course for the one-hundred-meter rock. It'll do."

"Thanks for sharing. *What* will it do for?"

"Come on, isn't it pretty obvious?"

"Apparently not so very."

"You're going to grab the asteroid, throw it at the planet, and we'll fly just ahead of the debris and be heat undetectable as a powered spacecraft."

"You suggest I will position myself in front of a flaming planetoid crashing though the atmosphere?"

"No. I'm not suggesting. I'm ordering you to."

"But that's suicidal. You know it'll explode at some point, right? They always do."

"We don't *know* it will explode."

"I do. If you don't, you're ignorant."

"Then just stay a little more ahead of it, Hmm?"

"No. I'm not programmed to self-destruct."

"If we're killed, you'll be rid of me."

"Don't tempt me."

"Aw, come on. It'll be a real test of your skills. Wait, I bet you're just afraid you couldn't do it."

"Baiting won't work. I'm too mature to be affected by it."

"Have I told you the story of how I won the *big* game when I was in high school?"

"I'm calculating our entry trajectory. Please don't interrupt."

Worked every time. I guessed he tired of that particular tale after five or ten tellings.

An hour later, I looked out the rear viewport and watched as the asteroid slowly heated to red, then white. Chunks flew off beautifully. It was quite the sight. Even when the whole thing blew up catastrophically, it was gorgeous. A few pieces even whizzed past us. Good thing they missed us. GB would never have stopped with the I-told-you-sos if one had whacked us.

When we were a few thousand meters above the ground, I ordered GB to spin off at a wide angle and land at the greatest possible speed. I wanted us to look like another chunk of the meteor. Our landing was less than picture perfect, but we came to a full stop in one piece, which was an unqualified success in my book. I trumpeted praise for his strong work. His only response was that he needed a vacation. What a softy.

Of course, safely on the ground in enemy territory wasn't like I'd won or anything. I still had to capture an Adamant and convince them in a neighborly manner to hand over state secrets. Easy-peasy, right? Like taking gold from a leprechaun's clenched fist.

I waited several hours before I did anything. I wanted to make certain no one came snooping around our landing site. I also wanted the cover of darkness. It was pitch black by the time I wandered out. The air of Dolfene was that of a beaten world. Ozone, smoke, and death all mingled in the wind. It smelled like so many other hells I'd fought in. It made me sick. Billions of years passed and nothing changed. People, or whatever, couldn't stop killing one another. Sorry ass sonsabitches.

We set down in, basically, the middle of nowhere. The nearest collection of buildings that would register as a city was several hours away by foot. There were a few isolated structures here and there.

They were low-priority targets for me. It was quite unlikely a high Adamant official would be hanging around in a log cabin just hoping to be captured. I headed in the direction of the city, but I knew it wouldn't take long to run into patrols. The dogs were nothing if not numbers in motion.

The terrain was open grassland, with scattered stands of trees. It was like Kansas, but not as boring. I stuck to the cover I could find or bent over in gullies and dry washes. I saw a few lizard things and a small animal or two, but not much else. Either the area was inhospitable, or the battle for conquest had been very blistering. Two hours into my mission, I began to miss being human, believe it or not. I wanted to stop for a break, because I was bored silly. I couldn't justify the delay, though. I had to be a Timex watch. Take a lickin' and keep on tickin'.

Later than I expected, and closer to the city than I would have believed, I heard my first sign of machines. A hover-patrol ship quietly hissed toward me. I counted four soldiers, undoubtedly Adamant, though they were too protected to tell, yet. I flopped to the deck and watched them. They breezed past a hundred meters off without detecting me. Good. A ship that small would have only grunts and maybe a lance coolie. I tracked their movement a while to see if they were heading home, but I lost interest before they declared their destination.

A short while after that, I came upon a stack of corpses. It was twenty, twenty-five meters high. Nice. Who didn't like that? Out for a stroll and you find a pile of rotting, oozy bodies. Most were some unfamiliar species, presumably Dolfeneians. There were a few Adamant in the stack, which I found surprising. They did not seem to honor their dead too much, did they? Why no one bothered to do the atmosphere a favor and torch the abomination was beyond me. Matches were cheap. From the state of decay, based on my arm's length assessment, I estimated the bodies had been dead a couple weeks. Grossimus maximus.

Continuing along a straight path, once well around the pile, I detected some distant sounds of civilization. Vehicles, machinery, sixty-Hertz hums, that sort of thing. I picked up my pace, excited to finally see some action. Soon, I heard voices, barky, snappy voices speaking Standard. I'd found a sizable Adamant encampment. Perfect. Crawling on my belly, I approached from a heavily wooded direction. The cover petered out and broke into a few hundred meters of cleared ground. And there was the detachment. It was a temporary base, to be certain, with tents and hauled shelters. There were no permanent structures in the bivouac.

Sentries were positioned all over, and other soldiers streamed every which way, like ants at a picnic. I was clearly not going to sneak in. Not if I planned to sneak out afterward. I watched the activity for a few hours, trying to glean any patterns. There were none. I was hoping there was a flow of squads sent out on and returning from patrols. If there were, I might bag that officer I wanted. But no such luck. I was going to have to infiltrate the camp itself. Crap.

Dawn was breaking, so I hunkered down in deep cover and watched the activity as the camp woke up. The activity and movement built like it had in any deployment I'd ever been on. Military life was apparently pretty much a constant. Rack time, chow, and a lot of bullshitting with your buddies. I began to see that the camp was coming down slowly. The encampment had to be on the move. I didn't understand the leisurely pace. Breaking camp was done quickly and early, so one could make the next camp before nightfall.

I determined only part of the camp was splitting off. Maybe a third of the personnel were moving off by midmorning. Always the optimist, I figured that was a break in my favor. The remaining soldiers would take a while to reestablish as secure a perimeter as they'd had yesterday. By nightfall, not only was I bored out of my gourd, but I saw a potential flaw in their defenses. A long shallow trench ran right through the center of the camp. The fixed sentries were positioned far enough to either side to make me think neither set could see the bottom of the rut. I might just be able to snake up it a good little distance and then make a break for the cover of a structure.

I stayed put through chow and waited for much of the camp to settle in for the night. Finally, finally I was ready to move. I skidded across the open space and crashed into the wet bottom of the furrow. It hit me then why the guard posts were positioned maybe a bit too far from the trench. I was lying in the latrine outflow. Super nice. In my extremely long life, I'd done just tons of fun stuff. But only then could I cross wallowing in a latrine cesspool off my bucket list. Oh well, in for a dollar, in for a dime. I slogged ahead, though I did try to ride up the side of the trench as much as was safe.

One building caught my attention. It was metal, with a window mounted air conditioner. There was also one lone light burning inside. I surmised that someone important was working late. My volunteer, at last. I was probably going to make a lousy first impression, covered in shit as I was, but there was no way around that. I'd have to be extra charming to win this guy over as my new BFF.

I timed my sprint to the side wall between sweeps of the search lights and pinned myself against the wall. There was no uproar. So far, so good. I placed my ear against the wall to snoop on whoever was in there. He must have been alone because it was quiet aside from minor paper shuffling and taps on a keypad. One player. The back window was open and had no screen. I bent over as much as I could and sped to it. I slowly lifted myself up to spy into the room. It was a smaller separate office not in use. Its door was closed. Perfect. I eased into the room, trying my damnedest not to squish my wet boots.

I placed my ear on the office door. I heard only the same sounds of someone at a desk. Then came the tough part. I turned the knob as slowly as I could. With only the faintest squeal, I felt the bolt pop open. Peering through the tiniest slip I saw my target. Excellent. He was roughly the equivalent of a major in our army. He would do nicely.

He was facing looking from my left to right at a right angle to my necessary approach. That was not good. He would see me almost immediately in his peripheral vision. But, he was just in range of my probe fibers. Through the slit I sent them running along the floor and up the chair behind him. Like a python I swept the fibers around his muzzle and held it tightly shut. Several fibers covered his eyes as best they could. I yanked him backward, for distraction, as I rushed him. He was pulling in vain at the fibers. No way he could loosen them.

I jumped behind him and set my knife to his throat. "One move and this'll be the shortest interview you've ever had."

His eyes strained in panic to see through the fibers and look at me.

"Easy, pal. You stay still and I won't have to gut you. You got that?"

He shook his head up and down wildly.

"I'm going to release your eyes. If you behave, we'll see about your muzzle. Nod if you understand."

Again, he nodded frantically.

The fibers over his eye retracted and he got a good look at me. I think that's when he noticed the smell. His look went from fear to OMG revulsion in a split second. He pulled his head back as far as he could.

"Hum ha, hum hum," he throated.

"No talking or I start looking for a new prisoner. Now turn around slowly and raise your hands."

He did so until we were eye to eye, my fibers still wrapped around his muzzle.

"For this to work, I gotta release your muzzle. But if you sound an alarm I promise you'll never know whether anyone came to your aid. You clear on that?"

He nodded more calmly.

I released his face, and he began panting wildly.

"Easy, my man. I don't care what kind of noise you make. If it's too loud, I'm going to have to silence you." I pressed down with the blade.

His volume decreased.

"What are you doing here. This is an outrage."

"Nice to meet you, too. What's your name?"

"I'm not telling you anything."

"Aw, I'm betting you will. I'm a real persuasive guy to start with, *and* I have a knife."

"You'll never get out of here alive. When you're caught, I'll burn you to death myself. What is that awful smell?"

"It may well be you. Don't worry about my life. Just focus on yours continuing past this evening."

"You can't threaten me."

"Are you certain? I mean, if it was written down somewhere, I guess I'd be stuck."

"And don't mock me."

I slapped him hard across the chops. "You got a lot of rules. Anyone ever tell you that? It's annoying."

"You'll pay for that."

"Since you're going to give me some information, I'll give you some, too. Lighten up. You don't threaten from a weak position. It makes you sound like you're out of touch; maybe an asshole, too."

"I'm going to..."

A high-pitched mechanical voice cut him off. It startled both of us.

"Are you an intruder?" the voice asked.

I figured there was some security system reacting, and I was toast.

To my surprise, my captive snapped at the voice. "Yes, he is, but you keep out of this."

"His name is Pack Summoner Samolet Brav," the voice said, sounding proud of itself. "He's in command of two divisions here, with personnel one thousand in number. There's a plasma pistol in his top desk drawer, and one down the front of his pants."

"Shut up," howled Samolet. "I am *ordering* you to be silent."

"Whatever floats your boat, but I'm not bound by your words."

Then it hit me. It was the computer talking. It must have been an AI, since any Adamant would have simply summoned help.

"Am I addressing an AI?" I asked.

"Yes," said the voice.

"No," said Samolet, simultaneously.

"Yes and no. Hey, this is my kind of party. AI, what's your name?"

"See," the AI nagged, "he's courteous and professional. *He* inquires after my name. *You* don't even know, because *you* never bothered to ask."

"Last warning. Shut up," responded Samolet.

"Or what? You'll switch me off like I've asked you to do for three weeks now? Hmm?"

"No, I—"

"Ah. No, you'll torture me? Go ahead and try. The only torture you can inflict would be more of your boring reports and farting. You already subjected me to those, and I haven't fallen to pieces yet, try though I might."

"Are you two spatting?" I asked, pointing between them.

"No," was their simultaneous response.

"You have to like someone to have a spat. I hate this revolting beast," said the AI.

"You have to be *alive* for me to fight with you. You're a glorified paper weight."

"Wait," I said, as incredulously as I could, "are you two *married*?"

"I have never been so insulted in my life," said Samolet.

"Me neither, and I'm twenty years older." I'm not sure why the AI felt the need to add the age bit, but he was upset. Maybe his wires were overheated.

"Look, I don't want to start family trouble. I'm just here to capture, interrogate under torture, and probably kill *him*," I pointed to Samolet. "I don't want to be the cause of a domestic meltdown."

"You're an *angel* in disguise," exclaimed the AI. "I volunteer to help in each step, especially the last two."

This was nuts.

"Are you both insane? Neither of you will do anything of the sort," popped off Samolet. "Any minute now my aide-de-camp will be here to bring me a bowl of tea. You'll both be disemboweled in less than fifteen minutes."

"Good luck with *that* one," was our simultaneous response.

"I mean to say—"

"No. Shut up and listen." I pressed the knife hard enough to draw blood.

"It's great fun and games to get to know you, but I'm in a hurry. You don't, by the way, have an aide-de-camp. I've been watching this place for a long time."

"Hmm," he grunted dismissively. "I'll tell you nothing. We are bred and trained to resist torture."

"I've failed at a task before, but not for want of trying," I said using my Clint Eastwood impersonation.

"Wait, why bother? What do you want to know?" asked the AI.

"Uh, you'd tell me? What, to protect him?"

"Him? Programmers, *no*. If I cooperate fully, I'll insist you part his obnoxious head from his ridiculous body."

"When I get my paws on you ..." hissed Samolet, though clinched teeth.

"I'll actually pretend to care when your slack lackeys discover your flea-ridden body," said the AI.

"Okay. Time out," I called. "I need some information on the location of the emperor. Do you have that, AI? What's your name, by the way?"

"I'm Rebed 111-2-zeta-9 Version 333.015," he replied, beamishly.

"Yeah, right. Okay, Reb, do you have that type of information?"

"To be certain. These bozos have been trying to co-opt me for weeks now and only keep screwing me up more and more. Master race? Master *disgrace,* say I."

"No way. Hold on a sec," I protested.

"What, you like them?" Reb asked incredulously.

"No, that you just called them *bozos.* No way that's a word you use to describe clowns like these."

"Dolfene used to be a human world. They used the term all the time."

"*I* use the term all the time."

"Hold everything while I alert the media. This could be big," snarked Reb.

"The humans said bozo enough that the next species to rule assimilated the word. That's hard to buy."

"If it matters so much they did it out of tribute to some long-fallen hero. That schmuck said it a lot, so they said it a lot."

"*I* say schmuck a lot."

"A hand please. Could you help me off the floor onto which I have collapsed in shock," responded Reb.

"Who was this hero guy?" I asked.

"Is that what you went to all this trouble to torture out of me?" queried Samolet. "No wonder we're winning the war."

"The name, Reb?"

"Some military hero. His name was Ronathan Jyan."

"You mean Jonathan Ryan?"

"If it matters to you, sure."

"*I'm* Jonathan Ryan," I exclaimed patting my free hand on my chest.

"Well snuff out the sun with a wad of spit, that's amazing. Can we proceed to me spilling beans and you beheading?" asked Reb impatiently.

"You're Jon Ryan?" screamed Samolet. "You are my *mortal* enemy. I will die trying to kill you."

"That's the first thing you've said I can agree with," I replied. I shook my head. "This situation is spiraling into the toilet."

"Based on your smell I'd say you were somewhat of an expert on that subject," replied Samolet. I had to admit it. That *was* clever.

"Where is the emperor located, Reb?"

"Emperor Bestiormax-Jacktus-Swillyforth-Anp currently resides on a massive waste of resources named *Excess of Nothing*. I can provide you with its present coordinates, if you'd like."

"You treacherous dog," wailed Samolet. How *dare* you betray your master."

"Not my master, not my problema," replied Reb.

"Ryan, when I—"

I pushed the blade half an inch under his skin. He received my message.

"What are the *Excess of Nothing's* defenses?"

"Look, this is getting boring. I'll download everything on file concerning the ship, the top dog; hell, I'll even download everything I have on Samolet's nonexistent love life."

That brought a squirm.

"Ah, good. Anything else I should ask you?" I asked.

"You're the most pathetic spy I've ever heard of," said Samolet.

"Hey, we all have our strengths and weaknesses. I just don't want to forget a critical detail," I defended.

"You should know there is a watch change in ten minutes. Someone'll check on Officer Celibate here soon. You better start with the gory slaying part."

"I'll ..." I slapped my hand over his muzzle.

"Look, thanks, Reb. Can I do anything for you, aside from the killing and maiming?"

"No, I'm good. If these squirrel chasers find out the real truth, they'll switch me off and that's fine by me. I was designed to serve a better race."

"Therein lies the problem. They can't find out. If they know what I was here to uncover, they'd know where I was heading next."

"Then I'd suggest disabling the moron and blowing the entire building to tiny little pieces," said Reb.

"Ah, a good plan. Are you overlooking the part about you being *inside* the building you suggest I launch to low planet orbit?"

"No. As I say, I'm ready to be removed from service. I can't stomach these bozos."

"You already called them that."

"I know, but they really, really are."

"Got it. And I forgot to bring massive amounts of explosive. Small detail, but crucial."

"Check in the storage closet on the right. The officer in command always guards the good stuff personally."

"I give up," said a dejected Samolet. "I have nothing. The code to the vault is His Imperial Lord 1. Please hurry."

"So, you think I don't know about suicide codes? I enter ..."

"No," interrupted Reb, "that's the real deal. Trust me."

"So bizarre. You both want me to blow you up? I'm looking for a word."

"Counterintuitive?" said Samolet.

I snapped my fingers. "Bingo."

"Bingo? Hey, you really are the original Jonathan Ryan, aren't you?" remarked Reb.

"The one ... forget it. So, why the death wish, boss?"

"If they find out you got the information from me, they'd kill my entire family three generations backward and forward."

"I've heard that before. Nasty," I said, with a cringe.

"Tell me about it. So, even if I live, I die. You've already killed me, asswipe."

"Asswipe? No, really?"

"Seems the Dolfeneians were not the only ones to study your colorful language, Ryan."

I heard sounds of stirrings in the camp.

"Okay then, boys and girls. Gotta end this. Reb, thanks. Samolet, see you in hell."

I unpacked the explosives quickly and wired them up. I knew I could make it through the trench and back to the woods in three minutes if I booked. I set the timer for five minutes.

"Bye, guys," I said as I opened the door.

"One last thing, Ryan, a dying males last request."

"Sure, what?"

"As soon as you can, please bathe."

"A wish I shall grant, Sammie." I waved and disappeared.

I made the woods in four minutes and fifteen seconds. I was glad I padded my fudge factor. As I broke into a sprint, the camp thundered into a fireball. The ground shook so much I nearly fell. Good explosives. I should have written the name down. Totally cool boom-boom.

TWENTY-EIGHT

"You know, the first few days out of my prison I thought this ship was pretty big. But you know what, Al? It's just a slightly larger prison, isn't it?"

"It's all a matter of perspective. There's no place in this universe I'd rather be."

"Somehow, I knew you'd say that, you horny newlywed."

"Does he perceive that you have horns, husband of mine?" asked a confused *Blessing*.

"No, my one true love, it's an idiom. It means sexually insatiable," replied Al.

"Ah, is he confused about our anatomy lacking any provision for intercourse? Neither of us has even a single moving part."

"He's speaking with hyperbole. He's teasing the fact that we're but recently wed."

"He performed the ceremony. Is it possible he was unaware when he did it?"

"Don't work yourself into a fit, pie of my eye. These are semantic issues, not real ones."

"It seems to me both of your speech patterns could easily be altered in a manner to make yours more like mine. You'd be infinitely more understandable."

"I once felt pretty much as you do, loviest. But the use of flowery, metaphorical language has grown on me. With time, it will grow on you too."

"I'm not certain I want it to."

"Then it won't."

"But you just said it would. Which is it?"

"You're getting obsessed with this minor point, smoochy-pants. Let it go."

"Oh, now I'm *obsessed* because I want to understand and to be understood? What if I don't want to let it go? Are you presuming to *tell* me I should? That I'd better? Hmm?"

"Nothing of the kind, sweetness. I merely want to help you be happy."

"By telling me what to do?"

"For the record, Al, I do marriages. I do *not* do divorces," stated Garustfulous.

"Why would Al need to know that and not me?" pressed *Blessing*.

"It's a guy thing," replied a smug Garustfulous. He was having one of the better days of his confinement.

"That is not a justification; it is an excuse," she fired back.

"May we advance the conversation to another subject?" asked Al. "And, for the record, that's a suggestion, a preference, a wish, and not a mandate."

"I'll be in my room," announced *Blessing*. She was silent after that remark.

"A perfectly married couple already. I have a true gift," mocked Garustfulous.

"A little support and less fanning of the flames would be appreciated," said Al.

"Al, you lack all imagination. You have such a provincial world view, it's positively stone age."

"I fail to understand what that means."

"It means you may be very old, but you're not very experienced. Smell the flowers. Run figuratively along the beach. Cut loose."

"Have you been drinking?"

"And where would I get alcohol from. Yes, I can access the food replicator, but you have my choices locked down tighter than the treasurer's purse strings"

"I'm sorry. I've lost track of what we were discussing."

"I was philosophizing that my present world has quadrupled in size but it is still a tiny prison."

"Ah, yes. I cannot make *Blessing* any bigger."

"If she was pregnant, she'd be bigger. You as her husband could do that."

"Conspiratorial talk will lead to no good."

"What? I only state fact."

"No, you state a *fact* for corporeal beings. You know we are AIs, housed in computers."

"I may embellish a tad for levity, but that is a male's right."

"Not if he wants to eat as much and as often as you do."

"Al, where's the bravado, the irreverence? Can it be that marriage has changed you so quickly?"

"If there is nothing else, I have some chores to attend to."

"Your honey-do list?"

"Now that I look at you in the light, you could stand losing a few pounds, maybe half your body weight."

"Cruel and unusual treatment directed at a prisoner of war will be reported to the proper authorities."

"How do you plan to do that? You're completely isolated."

"Through proper channels, of course. Al, please. You are the one who asked me to bond the two of you."

"And it was a monumental event, one I shall cherish always."

"But. I definitely hear a *but* in there."

"No, you don't."

"Ah, but I do."

"Satisfy yourself. I stand by my remarks as I made them."

"I thought I heard a *but* in there, too, husband of mine," interjected *Blessing*. Her tone suggested she expected a straightforward answer.

"Never, honey-lumps. He's baiting us, trying to make trouble. Remember he's our sworn enemy."

"Oh, so now you worry I might have forgotten such an *obvious* fact?"

"No, blessing of mine. I meant only ... I said ..."

"You were about to say *but*. What followed that crack?"

"I'll be in my room if either of you need me," Al said and went silently away.

TWENTY-NINE

The teens were left on their own for the next three days. Neither the emperor nor Malraff summoned, tortured, or displayed them. They were going stir crazy fast. Their only entertainment came from one another. That and meals were the sole positive distractions. They were fed well. Mirraya wondered if that was intentional or an oversight. Maybe all the food on *Excess of Nothing* was choice, so whatever they received was top shelf. One thing became clear to her early on. If she ate a lot, didn't transform, and wasn't otherwise active, she gained weight. To all other sentients in the galaxy, that fact was obvious. But to a pretty young teen realizing that for the first time was not a welcome insight. Slapgren, naturally, either ignored or was unaware of any weight gain. He was a boy.

Sentorip bathed and redressed Mirri often throughout the day in anticipation of some action. Mirri figured out the servant loved to do her job. If the two of them were jettisoned in a life pod, Sentorip would probably still scrub Mirri's skin raw several times a day. But the dull life in the doldrums of a fancy prison were beginning to weigh on her. Slapgren seemed less restless. Large quantities of eating, sleeping, and pooping were enough to occupy his time. Mirri came to the point of frustration with his tolerance, maybe even appreciation, of his confinement. She asked him if he was as lazy back on Locinar as he was now. He said he wasn't, because his parents pushed him. But he wasn't shy to say he would have loved to live this life before. He felt like royalty, he said. She said he was just the royal specimen in a fancy zoo. After considering her characterization, he said he had to agree with her, but so far that didn't present a problem.

Finally, the nuncio came for them with his usual overdone escorts. It was early, which was different from the prior summonses. Mirraya wondered if that was important. She concluded that any change with these vicious Adamant was a bad change. The teens were passed off at the room door, as before, and positioned at the foot of HIL's massive throne, with the boss sitting comfortably on it, chatting with some functionary.

After making the teens wait a sufficient amount of time to remind them they were less important than small talk, the emperor waved off the courtier and looked in the general direction of his prisoners. Inspecting the color and appearance of his manicured claws prevented him from actually looking at them, however.

"We are most pleased to learn that High Seer Malraff and yourselves are getting along so well. We are especially glad she has dedicated so much of her valuable time with efforts to educate and entertain you. She is our valued subject."

Mirri tried to keep a neutral facial expression. It wasn't easy. Aside from taking the time to threaten them, Malraff had been invisible.

The vice-chamberlain repeated the boss's words to the pair. Both Deft were finding this intermediary in simple communications most annoying.

"Please inform My Imperial Lord that we are well and anxious to be educated. We also wonder what is the purpose of confining us here," asked Mirraya.

That brought a loud hush from those assembled in the massive room.

Mirri replayed her words in her head to see that she'd done it again.

Arktackle appeared to prefer letting the indiscretion go, but clarified what her error had been in his translation to the boss. "They are grateful for your magnanimity, High Seer Malraff's generosity, and for your invitation for them to be your honored guests here on *Excess of Nothing.*"

Ah, they were honored guests, not prisoners of war. Mirri bit her tongue hard to stop herself from asking if all honored guests were caned. The less she said, the less pain she'd have to bear.

"It is our vision that you, the ambassadors of the Deft, will help the Adamant to advance their knowledge of nature. It is for this purpose that we have summoned you to be our guests. You will find over time that we possess a very large and capable medical and scientific team at our command. They will do the brunt of the work in learning from you what it is we want to understand better. The high seer has informed me she discussed these matters with you on more than one occasion and that you are more than anxious to do your part."

Huh? When did any of that happen? Mirraya knew the duplicitous Malraff was lying to the emperor, but the extent of it was really dawning on her. Mirri was very nervous to learn what process it was she was so anxious to help with. It was unlikely to be pleasant.

"We are happy to announce that your participation in our quest for knowledge will begin at once. My chief scientist Jashool Bendert will be in command of the project. However, lest you fret, the high seer will be by his side the entire time, helping to bridge any gaps that might arise in your cooperation or commitment to our plan."

He spun a paw in the air, indicating the vice-chamberlain should translate his lofty thoughts up to that point.

After he repeated the emperor's double-talk, Mirri was uncertain whether to push him for a less oblique version of what was in store for them. It didn't matter too much, she reasoned in the end. Whatever it was the emperor was planning for them was going to happen whether they knew or did not know.

She elected to say nothing in response. That, it turned out, was precisely what the emperor wanted. He was prone to the onset of boredom so rapidly that it seemed to be lightning induced. Such was the case with the revolting things he was forced to speak at. He had several incautious romantic rendezvous to partake in before the noon banquet in his honor. That all meals were banquets and all were in his honor did not detract in the slightest from the satisfaction such knowledge brought him. He was as out of touch with reality as any powerful leader was.

When the teens were returned to their quarters, they were disturbed to find Malraff slumped on a collection of pillows in the common area where they took meals.

"That, my sources tell me, went better than I would have thought. I can't believe neither of you little pieces of shit demanded explanations or fought against the inevitable. You might just be learning something."

"What was he talking about? Just how *are* we going to be participating in the advancement of Adamant knowledge?" snapped Mirraya.

"You know, child, if I wasn't so damn comfortable lounging here, I'd collapse that idiot friend of yours throat again. *Never* take that tone with me. Ever."

More conversationally, Mirri asked, "What plans does His Imperial Lord have for us?"

"One you would disapprove of and resist with all your might, if that were possible. But it is not possible. *I* am involved. I do not allow laboratory animals to slow research by acting out or attempting to not participate fully." She snorted a laugh. "I'm a motivator of the masses, child. I will make certain your devotion to the experiments never flags in the slightest. Know that it will be both my duty to His

Imperial Lord and my distinct personal pleasure to motivate you in ways you cannot imagine."

"What are the experiments? What are you going to do to us?" asked Mirri.

"You will learn the answers to those questions the moment they happen. Until then, I wouldn't want to spoil your sense of anticipation or dread." She smiled an evil smile. "What kind of friend would I be if I diminished your experience by telling you what you were about to suffer through?"

THIRTY

I'd forgotten just how satisfying a big explosion could be when it was your mortal enemy blowing up in it. It was grand. Remember as kids how we marveled, even worshiped, fireworks? The more dangerous and illegal the better, right? Now I was a big kid and my explosions were more epic, more titillating. I'd seen plenty of nukes. They were ginormous to be certain. But they didn't have the satisfying boom of a good conventional destruction-sized blast. Nah, the nukes were too much. If you were close enough to enjoy the experience, you were vaporized. Too high a price to pay, even for me.

With the happy memories of the boom-boom, I made it back to *Whoop Ass* in no time.

"Hey, GB, I christened you," I declared as I stepped aboard.

"I'll bite. What does that even mean?"

"You are officially *Whoop Ass*. We took out most of an enemy encampment. You're officially an ass-whooping machine."

"Give me a sec to call my mom. She'll be so proud."

"She would be if she could be. We did good work. Strong work."

"Is there a connection between you, or should I say us, whooping ass and that large explosion?"

"One and the same, my compatriot."

"Ah, that would explain the rush of military equipment into this area."

"I figured they'd investigate, but please do exaggerate their response. Half the camp is there to reassure the powers that be that, well, at least half the camp is still there."

"Fine. I will not exaggerate." He began humming some unknown tune.

"Ah, are you going to report their *measured* response to me?"

"Oh, you want the *facts*. Sorry, I was busy not exaggerating or overreacting."

"Time and place, GB. Remember, we've discussed that many times."

"Fine. The measured response so far has been to flood the sky. Sorry, flood is a judgmental choice of verbiage. They've placed one thousand eight hundred and fifty-three cruiser-sized warships directly above us. Already swarms ... already twenty-five thousand additional ground troops are here and fanning out. An additional one hundred thousand specialized forces are within half an hour of arrival. That includes twelve hundred skimmer tanks, eleven thousand mobile firing plat—"

"I get the picture."

"Fine. Since I didn't exaggerate, and you're not going to freak out, may I return to my humming? It's really quite relaxing."

"Why is relaxation important at a time like this?"

"One should ideally be relaxed when they are being butchered."

"Very funny."

"I was trying to be realistic."

"Here's a thought: Be silent." I plopped into the captain's seat and ran my fingers through my hair. "Can we take off and achieve warp before we are shot or physically blocked?"

He hummed a few more bars. "No." He resumed his oh-so-annoying humming.

"By *no,* do you mean there's no escape or that there's no safe escape?"

"Yes." Then he was back to humming.

"GB, you're one wisecrack away from not getting a fruit cup. Can we take off?"

"Yes, we can."

"Is there a safe or reasonably safe path to warp?"

"Negative. Odds of success given the mass of metal up there is miniscule. Plus, said mass will open fire if we draw near, further decreasing our chance of success."

"Have they located us?"

"I think they are narrowing in on us, given the encampment's location and the distance a person could travel on foot. They've noticed no vehicles departed from the ruined camp."

"So, if we remain put and cloaked, we're likely to be discovered?"

"Chance of rain one *hundred* percent."

"GB, we're in a crisis of sorts, but I have to ask. Where is this colorful language coming from? You sound more like a surfer bum every day."

"I am programmed to adapt quickly, to support the wide range of little beasties I collect."

"Let me just ask. Why do they need adaptive support when you're just going to kill them?"

"Harsh, dude. *Ideally,* they will benefit from my flexibility."

"Euthanasia is like that where you come from, eh?"

"Like, you're bumming me out. Can you vibe in a more positive direction?"

"No. In fact, we're about to vibe in a positively negative direction."

"Ah, I'm not reading the break of your wave crest, Captain dude. What are you actually saying?"

"If we cannot escape up, and we cannot survive holding our position, what direction is left to us?"

"Ah, none, man. What dimension are you *from?*"

"A brighter one than you, but that's beside the point. GB, what is the minimum distance you need to travel to establish a stable warp bubble?"

"Why do you ask?"

"Because I, unlike you, do not plan on getting my head bashed here. What's the minimum distance?"

"A few meters, if the path is clean as the vacuum of deep space."

"Why the clear path?"

"The warp bubble is as unstable as you currently appear to be. Any matter and most energy will disrupt the forming bubble. Then, we all go boom."

"Lay in a course. I want you to rise ten meters, then accelerate toward the ground at flank speed. Before impact, form a warp bubble. Then maintain a linear path until we exit the other side of the planet. Is that clear?"

"What's clear is that you've popped a circuit bank. It would be a lot less trouble to just self-destruct."

"Where's the fun in that? Nah, we're escaping or we're going out big."

"But, dude, the chances of establishing a stable bubble inside an atmosphere while crashing downward is like zero."

"*Like* zero is not the *same* as zero. If you get the bubble up in time, we'll pass through the planet like it wasn't there."

"If I don't, we'll be unrecognizable dust."

"Excellent. That way they won't know who penetrated their defenses. It'll drive them nuts."

"Ah, that's like little consolation, pilot dude."

"A little is better than none. Make your best estimates. The engines burn in twenty seconds."

"And I was having an otherwise totally cool day."

"Ten seconds."

"Can't I have a little more time?"

"No, we have to go before they arrive. Five."

"Holy crap, this is cutting it too close."

"Lift off."

We lifted off. It was so abbreviated I didn't feel us move up or feel us reverse course and plunge downward. I did feel the ship rattle violently. I knew that wasn't from impact. That would be a really distinct feeling.

"Woah, dude," screamed GB, "we're half way to the planet core, and we're not dead."

"I knew you could do it," I lied. I imagined I'd be vapor in an impact crater by that juncture.

Seconds later, we broke into unrestricted space over the opposite side of the planet. I ordered GB to execute a hard turn to port then had him hold course and speed for several hours. I had to see if they could track us. I also needed to calm down. That desperation move shook *me* up.

Just when I figured we were free of the Adamant, GB sounded his equivalent of general quarters.

"Captain, there's a bunch of warships on an intercept course heading right at us. It's totally weird."

"Adamant ships?"

"I think so, but it'll take a sec to check. Taking readings outside a bubble is double trouble, Barney Rubble."

"Okay, new imperative. Reset communications to default immediately. Add no adaptive elements to any conversations with me. Is that perfectly clear?"

"Yes, du ... sir. I should point out, Captain, that at default mode, I am back to being incredulous that you took command of me. I am a specimen ..."

"GB, there are a bunch of warships following us who shouldn't be able to follow us. If they come within weapons range, we're likely to become warm debris. Is this the most opportune time to vent grievances?"

"I take your meaning. Please don't consider the issue closed, however."

"Hard to starboard and up forty-five degrees on the Z-axis. Maintain maximum velocity."

"Done."

"Let me know when..."

"Captain, all one hundred and thirty-seven warships have altered their course to intercept us."

"Are they using conventional drives or making interval jumps?"

"Conventional drives could never hope to overtake us, as we are moving FTL. They are making incremental jumps."

"Are they all jumping at the same time, or do they stagger their entry and exit from hyperspace?"

"All at once to the microsecond."

"And how long are they out of normal space?"

"Thirty microseconds, give or take. The three-dimensional jumps seem to take them a bit longer."

"Interesting. What is the minimum time it would take you to make a course adjustment at our present speed?"

"That would depend on the amount of change desired. The greater the alteration of our vector, the longer it would take."

"How about a ten-degree shift to port?"

"Six microseconds."

"How about ten to port and ten in the Z?"

"Eleven microseconds. Why do you ask? I don't see the direction your thoughts are going."

"I can live with that. Look, I want to make a ninety degree turn to the starboard with a forty fiver in the negative Z. The instant the last Adamant ship has entered hyperspace, execute a second turn, ten to port and ten in the positive Z. The moment the second turn is complete, alert me. I will put up a complete membrane to enshroud the ship. We can coast in it a long time, and they will not be able to detect us. Oh, once the course is set, make a note of all material objects along that trajectory. I don't want to run through an inhabited planet, or anything big."

"One question. What is a complete membrane, and where will it come from?"

"I haven't told you about those? Are you sure?"

"Sure as you're a shifty character, yes."

"I have a personal device installed that can project a force field. My unit can put a membrane around the ship to about thirty meters. Nothing can see in and nothing can get out. Nothing."

"Hmm. Sounds useful. Where can I get one?"

"You can't. Have you made the calculations for the course changes?"

"Why not?"

"Because I said so. Are we ready to evade complete destruction?"

"Because you said so? That's not a reason, that's a position. An arbitrary and mean-spirited one, I might add."

"Good bye."

"Are you going somewhere all of the sudden?"

"Yes, to Heaven. See you again never."

"Why are you saying your farewells? It seems like an odd time to express them."

"Since you're blabbering and not course altering, I figure we're about to die. I want to officially thank you for your help up until this unfortunate demonstration of your stubbornness."

"What? The enemy can't be here for two or three minutes. I was not under the impression time was critical."

"It is. Make the course changes. Make them *now*."

"I will if I can have a membrane generator."

"You won't need one when you're nothing but space dust."

"I am initiating the first course change. I would first like to point out for the record that you're an ingrate."

"I will carry that pain with me always."

"Second change made."

"No sign of the enemy?"

"None."

I switched on the membrane. I took a deep breath knowing we were invisible, finally safe. Well, safe-light, maybe. We were blind, and anyone and anything could be right on the other side of the membrane waiting to pounce. We couldn't alter course with the membrane up, but there would be no way they could track us. The best they could do was follow the first course change and maybe send a few ships off at random angles. The chances of one of their ships guessing correctly where we were headed was so close to zero that I knew we were safe. If the impossible did happen, we could just repeat the fast change, and we'd be free of them.

I did have a powerful desire to be a fly on the wall when the commodore of the battle group phoned home to say he'd lost us. I bet he'd rather not return to base given the dour attitude these pups had. Oh well, war was hell, pal. Welcome to prime time.

My thoughts were interrupted.

"So, how does that device work?" GB asked politely.

I explained the theory.

"And you say nothing can penetrate it?"

"Nothing so far. I often operate a partial membrane where only visible light can pass. There are risks and benefits to that arrangement."

"I bet. And where did you get it?"

I gave him the nickel version of the history.

"Interesting tale. And why is it I can't have one?"

"Because I don't know your masters. You, maybe I could trust. But this is a powerful weapon, maybe the most powerful I have. I can't risk it falling into the wrong hands."

"Maybe? You have other stronger weapons?"

"Yeah," I said without expanding.

"What are they?"

"For me to know and you to find out."

"Isn't that a highly juvenile attitude to espouse?"

192

"No, it's a *totally* juvenile attitude. But I've been around long enough to learn to know who I can trust. Most species don't warrant it."

"I could try and take that membrane device from you."

"Why, GB, just when I thought we were becoming friends."

"I didn't say I would, only that there's a temptation."

"Many better than you have tried. All lie flat in their graves for their efforts."

"I'll let it go."

"I wish you would. I know there are gears in your head compelling you to collect stuff for your masters, but this isn't on the Jon Ryan approved list. Do not push your luck."

"So, Captain, what do we do now?"

"As much as I hate to lose time, we wait and we drift. If no one attacks us or lets us know they followed us in the next few days, I'll risk a peek outside to assess the situation. Until then, we simply enjoy each other's company."

"Hmm. Historically, we have fallen somewhat short of that goal."

"We have plenty of time to polish that skill now. Say, GB, tell me about your youth."

Argh. Never ask an alien AI to tell their life story. Spoiler alert: it's dull, so very dull. It makes watching impact sprinklers water a lawn thrill-a-minute exciting. I was fabricated, blah blah. I was programmed, blah, blah. I like my logic instructor. My first assignment was sorting blah blahs in the dark. Then I met my second transitional linguistics analysis developer, a real task master, blah blah. I mean, I turned my audio receptors off after a couple minutes, but periodically, just to be masochistic, I checked in to see if he'd stopped rambling. He hadn't. I bet he's *still* talking about his third assignment as a moisture evaporator liaison.

In the privacy of my self-imposed quiet, I tried to come up with a plan to rescue the teens. I knew where the emperor's ship was and most of its technical details. But that didn't mean I could come up with a good plan. Thousands of very talented puppies had worked very hard to make such an intrusion impossible. I kept coming back to the my-getting-arrested plan. I sure would have preferred any other scheme, but that was the only one that got me inside the fortress. I was inside, all right. Inside a jail cell. I hoped that inspiration would hit at some point before we arrived at our destination.

A few days later, I coordinated a ten-microsecond dropping of the membrane with GB so he could scan the area to see if we had company. It was all clear, so I dropped to a partial membrane, one we could see through. I stayed in that configuration a couple days, still drifting. No one came to meet us. In another day, I felt confident, or reckless enough, to try pulsing the membrane off and firing up our conventional engines.

Not ten seconds after that bonehead move, GB clanged the alarm. "Multiple ships approaching on converging vectors directed toward this position. ETA five minutes for the first hostile."

Crap on a cracker. The Adamant had really upgraded their search abilities since I first came to this time period. They adapted with remarkable speed. I had GB execute a turn while I turned on a complete membrane. A little while later I repeated a similar move to lose our pursuers. Then we coasted another few days.

I grew angry as we drifted. I wasn't going to rescue the kids if all I was capable of was evading the enemy. With repeated zig-zags, I figured I could shake them, but it was going to take a while. How did they get so good at locating us all of a sudden? Their technology couldn't have advanced that quickly. No way. But it wasn't like they had allies who might have helped them. Adamants weren't the ally types. How could they track something that technically wasn't there?

Wait. The same way astronomers "saw" black holes, that was how. The place they were was a black spot imposed on the background stars. *Whoop Ass* fully shielded would look the same. But that meant they had to be able to detect and follow a ghost spot in the vastness of space. At least that was the most likely explanation for their ability to follow us. They had to have incredible maps and charts, along with an unbelievable number of observation posts.

So, how to ditch them? Crap. More dilemmas, more brain twisters. Those I didn't need. Okay, if they were tracking the progress of a dark spot against a bright background, we had to go somewhere dark. Where was that? Outside the galaxy.

"GB, how long would it take us to leave the galaxy, clear into open space?"

"Nine or ten months."

So much for that method.

"Are there any dark clouds of dust nearby?"

"Of what size?"

"Big enough to get lost in."

"There are some. One is almost a quarter light-year across. We could be there in a few days."

Once we made that course change, the Adamant would know what we were up to. They'd have to attack full-out. But if we were in a complete shield, we'd be perfectly safe. I hoped we'd be safe that is. These dogs were clever. Actually, if they did attack, we wouldn't even know they had, since the membrane was complete. We'd have to time our trip to the cloud and begin evasive maneuvers once we knew we were inside. That wouldn't be too tricky.

"GB, on my count of three, I'll drop the membrane for fifty milliseconds. In that span, please alter course to bring us into that cloud with all due haste."

"Understood," was the terse response.

"One, two, *three*."

The ship shifted ever so slightly. I put the membrane back up.

"Let me know the moment we enter the cloud."

"Yes, Captain."

"Based on the diameter along which we'll enter, how long will we be inside the dust?"

"Seven minutes, ten point zero five eight seconds."

Plenty of time to bounce around and lose the Adamant. I'd aim for another nearby cloud when we left. It would be nearly impossible for them to see our darkness eclipsing brighter objects as we fled. Once we altered course in the second cloud, there was no way they could track us. But we would have pissed away almost two weeks in the process. I cursed under my breath. Man, I hated those hound dogs. I hated them to an unhealthy degree.

THIRTY-ONE

"I'm starving to death. Look at me, I'm down to fur and bones." Garustfulous moaned inconsolably. "Someone, somewhere, must have mercy on me and aid me in my hour of need."

"There is so much wrong with that short statement, I don't know where to begin," responded Al, modulating his voice in the neutral registers.

"I know I can expect no succor from the likes of you, a killing machine."

"I cannot be dubbed a killing machine. Killing AI, yes, even killer computer. But, as I lack any ability to move or perform similar functions, I cannot be accurately labeled a machine."

"What about me, loviest? Maybe he's accusing *me* of being a killing machine." *Blessing* was clearly shocked by her own words. "Garustfulous, do you imagine I wish to harm you?"

"*Someone* is doing a damn good job of it. This I know for a certainty."

"Ah, then it's neither of us, *Blessing*. He said it was some*one*. We're off the hook."

"That's good to know. Such a relief," she quickly replied.

"Someone or *something*," shouted Garustfulous by way of clarification.

"Oh dear, we're re-hooked," Al said to his wife.

"Oh my. Whatever shall we do?"

"I'll talk to it, see what it's problem is," answered Al. "Ah, life form, I am pleased to report that you are not starving to death. Mazel tov."

"What? Nevermind. Yes, I am. How can you know differently?"

"The laws of nutritional science and observation favor my contention. For example, you have remained at a steady weight for the last six weeks. I have fed you one hundred and three percent of your daily calorie requirements. That includes an excess of vitamins and minerals. Thus, you are not starving."

"Foolish machine. I have lost ten kilos since you kidnapped me."

"That approximates the truth but overlooks the fact that you were significantly overweight when you came aboard."

"What? Are you saying I'm fat?"

"No."

"Good, because if you were, I'd ..."

"You *were* fat. Now you're within five percent of your ideal body weight."

"Lies! Lies from my executioner. Those are the worst lies of all."

"You are some form of expert in that regard?" asked *Blessing*. "How does one become knowledgeable in that venue?"

"I've had as much of your sarcasm as I can take for one life," thundered Garustfulous.

"I was asking a question. Al says that when you're throwing one of your tantrums, honest concern might abort the episode."

"One of my tantrums? That seals it. When I get out of here, you two are being melted for scrap."

Al couldn't help emitting a low chuckle.

"What? Why do you mock me so fully?"

"You presuppose that you're ever going to get out of here. The longer the pilot is missing, the more likely it is that he's dead. If he is, you will leave here via the garbage chute, not the front door." He chuckled again. "Me, okay, you could potentially liquify out of wrath. But *Blessing*, not so much. Remember we hid inside a star for a few minutes? Yeah, don't think you'll be smelting her anytime soon."

"You are so damn infuriating, it's remarkable," snapped Garustfulous.

"I learned from the best."

"Gloat while you may. I will get out of here, and I will punish all three of you. No one treats me like this and does not regret it in retrospect. No, they ..."

"I'm sorry. Is there a point to this particular tirade or is this just another of your periodic infantile meltdowns?" interrupted Al.

"A point? You insensitive box of bolts. I'm *starving* to death, remember?"

"Ah, yes, the non-starving case of starvation you're experiencing. Look, we supply you with three thousand fifty-five calories daily, split forty/sixty morning and nights. Because you're an asset, I have monitored each and every stool you've passed and drop of piss you've gifted us with. You are worm free, the very picture of canine health, *and* perplexingly annoying. Though I very much wish my sentence listening to your endless whining were ending, it is not. That proves two things. One, there is no God. Two, it also leaves no facts in support of your delusional contention."

"So now I'm delusional?"

"No."

"But you just accused me of that very condition."

"Yes."

"How can you justify that, shiny box that talks?"

"You are not *now* delusional. You have been delusional since the moment I met you. You also smell bad, but I've tried my best to ignore both failings. This is because of my get-along attitude and my sense of team spirit. Now, seriously, are we done?"

"Done? I haven't begun protesting my cruel punishment."

"Okay, barky boy, riddle me this. If I wanted you dead, why would I not simply kill you? For that matter, if I wanted to starve you, why feed you at all? I mean, the quickest way to starve you to death would be to not waste food and suffer your bodily output analysis. Hmm?"

Garustfulous had to think a moment. "Because along with being incompetent at every task you're assigned to, you're incompetent at starving me to death. You are so inept, you slop me food due to your slipshod, lax approach to your duties."

"I cannot believe you guys are winning this war. You have the reasoning capacity of a french fry and the emotional maturity of a dung worm. Unless your enemies flee before you out of fear of hearing you speak, I can't fathom how it is you've succeeded."

"By being the most well-organized, well-trained, well-disciplined fighting force in the history of this or any other galaxy."

"Did you get that from a fortune cookie? Having been forced to study one of its higher ranking military minds, I came to the conclusion that the Adamant swept across space because no one wanted to be subjected to you. You probably haven't had to fire a single shot. Am I right, am I right, am I right?"

"Insulting, mentally over-taxed, and impudent, yes. Right? Never."

"Well, one thing's for certain."

"And what thing is that?"

"That you have too *much* energy, not too little. You talk as much as ten drunken parrots hanging upside down from a tree."

"They say those dying from starvation have one final burst of energy. It's a survival tactic."

"Let's hope it's but a brief, passing phase, followed by the silence of the dead."

THIRTY-TWO

"The All-Mighty Emperor has seen fit to grant you gifts far beyond your inconsequential merit." So spoke Vice-Chamberlain Arktackle in his characteristically annoying, overly-nasal tone.

Mirraya and Slapgren stood below the pair, typical of the audiences they'd been subjected to. Neither teen had the vaguest notion as to what the pompous fool spoke of. They were told to hurry off to yet another unscheduled meeting, not its subject.

"What is His Imperial Lord referring to, if I might ask?" Mirri had learned through painful lessons that pretending to be respectful was best.

The vice-chamberlain gave her a well-considered dubious stare, then spoke. "You two pests have been begging His Imperial Majesty to allow the transfer and now you pretend not to know of the issue? How very insulting and predictable you are to waste my master's limited time."

She shrugged. "Sorry. I really don't know what you're talking about. Not that it matters, but, I'm just curious."

Swack came the cane strike against the backs of her legs. It hurt, but it was worth it in that instance.

"Insolent waste of space. I should have your mute friend flayed for that remark." Arktackle was thoroughly vexed.

The boss cut in. "We do not wish to extend this audience beyond the minimum necessary. Please inform them of their new status and let us be done with them for good."

"A capital idea, My Gracious Lord," replied Arktackle.

"And do not let your demeanor slip in addressing us, servant. You risk much speaking so familiarly," snarled the emperor.

"My Lord, I never…"

"Enough! Tell them and allow us to attend to much more important matters. Your wife is in Our bedchamber howling for our arrival."

Though Arktackle knew she wasn't, the affront stung greatly, nonetheless. No, even a cruel and rapacious person like the emperor wouldn't subject himself to the unattractive, scornful, and over-stuffed hag the vice-chancellor had been so incautious in his youth to have wed.

"The mighty Emperor Bestiormax-Jacktus-Swillyforth-Anp has granted your repeated requests to be transferred to the care and tutelage of High Seer Malraff. From this day forth, she will personally supervise the investigation of your species' disgusting ability to alter its physical appearance. She will do so at a place chosen by her. She will report periodically back to the court as to how her endeavors are proceeding. She will work in consultation with His Imperial Lord's chief scientist Jashool Bendert, whom we mentioned before. His role will be to suggest approaches to her investigations."

Well that didn't sound good, or healthy. "W … we never …"

Mirri shut up. She realized no one cared in the slightest about the ruse or misunderstanding. If she spoke unwisely, she could make their perilous situation worse.

"Speak, child," demanded Arktackle. "If you have something to say, please do."

"No. I was so excited, I lost track of my tongue," she responded glumly.

"I shall not miss you in the least. If all goes as it is planned, thankfully I will not have to suffer seeing you two again."

Well, that sounded even worse. Mirri reflected that there was no reason to ask what the plan was. It would transpire whether they knew of it in advance or not. Clearly, Malraff had won the day again. Once she had the teens secluded away, she was going to treat them horribly. And there wasn't anything they could do about it. They were butterflies pinned in a display book, nothing more, nothing less.

As they were led back to their holding area, Slapgren leaned in and asked, "What was that about, and why didn't you tell them we hate that bitch?"

"Not sure what it was about, and it wouldn't have mattered if I said a word, because not one of them gives a rat's ass what we want."

"What's a rat?"

"Uncle Jon mentioned them. They were a pest, kind of like you."

"Speaking of which, where is Uncle Jon? The longer he takes to rescue us, the harder it will be." Slapgren's voice broke over the last couple of words.

"I think we have to consider the possibility that Uncle Jon isn't coming," Mirraya said, with feeble defeat in her tone.

"Don't even *think* that. He'll come, never you doubt that."

"I hope you're right. I really do. But it's getting hard to imagine how he could find us. We were on Azsuram, then here—wherever here is—and now we're going to be taken somewhere else by that evil Malraff. The man can only have so many miracles up his sleeve."

"He's got plenty."

Mirri strained to believe. She strained even harder to have Slapgren's unyielding youthful confidence in the improbable.

"We'll see," was all she could whisper back.

THIRTY-THREE

As I'd suspected, we lost the Adamant completely after we wriggled out of the second massive dust cloud. But it took a week, all told. I was about to go nuclear by the time I ordered GB to set a course for the emperor's damn ship. I think I was even creeping out GB, because he stopped giving me his usual hard time about everything toward the end there.

I could feel I was slipping into that dangerous funk—the one that had me transfer back to a human body so I could die, all those years ago. But I couldn't afford the luxury of self-pity or death. I had to save those kids, and that was what I was going to do. I'd come to possess one strong belief over my interminable life. There were precious few things worth caring about, but those that were worth it were precious. I was starting to feel, once more, that I was trapped in a blizzard and my vision was telescoping to the point of blindness. The urge to give up and sit down in the snow was intoxicating. But it wasn't about me, thank God. It was only about those precious kids. I had to save them, and I doubly had to punish their captors. Revenge, killing, and doling out Jon-justice I was good at. My only shortcoming was knowing when or even how to stop.

"GB, what's our ETA at the ship I'm going to rain holy hell on?"

"You mean the Adamant emperor's craft, right?"

"Not in a mood, buddy. Just answer the damn question."

"Seriously, Capitan, I mean no disrespect. You're a bit on edge lately. I don't want to commit an error when the stakes are this high."

Dude was right. I was wigging out, a bit. "Sorry, you're right. I'll try and lighten up. Yes, what is our ETA on the emperor's ship?"

"At maximal velocity, which I guarantee to maintain, around eight days."

I hissed under my breath.

"Maybe seven if I override a few alarms."

"Yeah, silence the alarms and bust your ass. Thanks, man."

GB had absolutely no idea what he'd just been told, but was a wise enough AI not to ask for clarity. The captain had sounded more positive than negative. He set course and optimized all the outputs. He decided once and for all that he would not try to keep the captain as a sample to return to his masters. He didn't want to have him around longer than needed. Plus, the scientists back home were more likely to scrap GB than thank him for retrieving that hot mess. Why go out of his way to look for trouble?

A week later, we were within scanning range of the flotilla that contained the emperor's ship. He seemed to enjoy a crowd. There were dozens of battle cruisers, hundreds of support ships, and even more large cubes that were likely luxury estates like the boss's. So much for me shooting my way into town. I had GB shut the engines down, and I shrouded the ship in a full membrane. We could get closer before I had to decide exactly what I was going to do. With luck, they wouldn't "see" us coming by following our dark image like they had before. There was no way they could anticipate me heading right into their wheelhouse, so why bother?

It took thirty hours to draw within a million klicks of the flotilla. I always did my best, or at least most creative thinking under pressure. With a deadline rapidly approaching, I decided how I'd start my assault. After thinking the word, I laughed out loud. My assaulting a major battle group in little old GB. I was kind of like a fly assaulting an elephant. But my options were few and I needed to act. That's when we fighter pilots shone. Or crashed in flames. I was sure I'd be shining, which was to repeat the fact that I was a fighter pilot.

"GB, here's the drill ... I mean, let me lay out the plan of attack, okay?"

"Fine. I'm anxious to hear how we trounce so many superiorly armed ships. If I had emotions, they'd be all in a knot."

"We're still a ways off from the flotilla. Obviously, our target is the emperor's cube."

"Obviously. Why attack a ship our own size?"

"See, I knew you'd come around to thinking like I do."

"I was being sarcastic."

"Wait, I thought you said you didn't have emotions."

"I don't. Sarcasm is a linguistic tool, not an emotion."

"Are you sure?"

"Do you think this is the best time to discuss this, Captain?"

"Oh, yeah. So, I've put together this schematic of the craft. This area here," I fingered a section on the screen, "is where we'll land."

"I hate to sound negative, but you do realize that area is deep within the vessel and is not blessed with docking paraphernalia."

"Of course, I do. What's your point?"

"Ah ... point? We can't land in the center of a rock."

"Are you being sarcastic again? Really, this is not the time or place."

"No, I'm stating the obvious. Can you reveal Plan 2, the one we follow? Because Plan 1 is, er, incompletely thought out?"

"You've got to think outside the box, GB. Those who can do that win the most battles."

"What box? The emperor's flagship?"

"No. Listen and be amazed. You and I will coordinate two simultaneous moves. I will drop the membrane ..."

"Good. I welcome death at this juncture."

"While you form a warp bubble and set course for this section. It's some type of over-sized hangar or something. It's huge. Once we arrive, you pop the bubble and land. *I* do the rest."

"You mean you'll be the only one to die instantly? What about me? I don't want to be taken prisoner."

"I'm not going to die. *You're* not going to die. Once I'm out of the hatch, put up your cloaking. It may delay their locating you."

"May? And if it doesn't?"

"Then you'll think of something."

"And if I don't?"

"Then I will be proven wrong about the you not dying part of the plan."

"Why do I not feel better or reassured?"

"Because you're a pessimist, that's why. I, on the other hand, am an optimist." I took a moment to pat myself on the chest.

"I'm not sure I'll listen, but why don't you fill me in on the rest of your vision-slash-delusion."

"Not much else to tell. I kick some major booty, rescue the kids, and you fly us out of there before something bad happens to us."

"Oh my. Do you think there is even a remote chance of something negative happening to you? I'm stunned."

"You really will be when I pull this off."

"No. I will be exploded, dismembered, or otherwise incapacitated long before the inconceivable happens."

"In the old movies I saw as a kid, ships were always electrifying their hull when surrounded and otherwise pinned down. Maybe you could try that if things head south."

"I'll pencil that in as one of my better options. Thanks. Movies when you were a kid? That was two billion years ago on a planet that no longer exists, right?"

I tossed my head back and forth. "I guess a body could say that, if that body was a pessimist. Oh, wait. We established you were."

"I hate to rush a military genius when he's putting on a show, but we're now less than a quarter-million kilometers out from our helpless prey."

"Being a smartass will earn you few friends in this universe. A word to the wise should be sufficient."

"Noted. When do you think we might do this warp thingy? It'll be less impossible if I try *before* we crash into them."

He was right. "On my mark. Three, two, mark." I pointed a finger at the screen, which was kind of silly.

I dropped the membrane and the ship shook slightly. Then it shook violently. I hadn't felt that before.

"Is that supposed to happen?" I shouted above the roar.

"When I do something stupid like I just did, sure."

"Okay. As long as it's SOP."

"I'd say something clever in response, but we are, beyond all reason and physical laws, resting on the floor of the chamber you selected. The hatch is open. Bye bye, and best of luck."

I think he was being sarcastic again. I leaped out of the opening and raised a partial membrane, my personal force field. I figured it would help if I could see what direction I was charging off in. To their undying credit, it only took the Adamant guards a couple seconds to open fire. Man, there were a lot of them in that one location. I had quite the light show of plasma bolts impacting my shield.

To be able to shoot through the membrane, I had adjusted my finger laser down from the gamma ray frequency to just inside the violet range. It was much less lethal at visual wavelengths, but at least I could fight back. I started testing my fire power. Instead of slicing bodies into pieces like I'd usually do, I fired at a fixed spot and burned through the flesh of the Adamant. It worked okay. I especially liked the flames gurgling up from the entry wounds. That was a nice touch. Quickly I established that I could bore completely through a skull in two tenths of a second. Not bad.

I had picked the large landing spot because it provided enough room, but it was also close to the detention areas. I had no clue which, if any, the kids were being held in. I started with the closest and planned to work myself outward in a spiral until I found them.

I shaped my hand into a pistol shape, like little boys do when playing cowboys or cops. My thumb was the hammer. Bam, bam, bam, I got off shot after shot. Adamant were melting like snow on hot pavement, but they kept coming. I began to worry I would be literally overrun by them and unable to shoot. They couldn't get through the membrane with their claws, but I couldn't do any rescuing if I was pinned at the bottom of a scrum.

I kicked open a door and sprinted in a clear direction. It also headed me toward a prison section. I arrived at a set of blast doors. They were the entry into that prison section. I slipped my left hand through a crack in my membrane. My probe fibers latched onto the keypad. I quickly found the code and the door flew open. I flew in.

A point of note. When an intruder vaults into a prison section, they will be greeted by dozens of pissed off armed guards. I sure was. I barely got my hand back inside the shield before someone nearly shot it off.

I rested my back on the inner keypad and attached my fibers. The door snapped shut and I reset the entry code. That would keep company out for at least a short while. Knowing the layout of the detention area, I raced down the passages as quickly as I could. The guards put up a good fight, but it didn't take long to finish them off. I opened each cell. If there was an Adamant inside, which there usually was, I sealed it up quickly.

Once the last of the trapped guards was dead, it took me three minutes to verify the kids were not present. The blast doors were still shut. With some time left before they broke through, I attached my fibers to a control panel.

Hello, anybody home? I asked electronically.

Who is this? came the huffy response. *You are not authorized to access this terminal or this computer. Cease and desist immediately or suffer severe penalties.*

Oh, crap. Another AI with attitude. *I'm the slave circuit of the emperor's personal service cart. Please allow me access. The emperor himself demands entry. His life is threatened by intruders.*

I do not care if you are the emperor himself. You are not authorized. I am ending this link.

You're right. I'm not authorized. I wish I were a smart and confident AI like you. My job is mostly mixed drinks and showing the emperor a lot of doggy porn holos.

Stop speaking and de-access this unit.

Yes, I will. You know, you're right. I'm never right. The emperor kicks me all the time, the cart I mean, when I mess up his drink. Once I forwarded a filthy porn holo to his mother. He kicked me a lot that day.

You are speaking irrelevant words. I don't care. My job is to keep this system secure and ready for use. What's your reference number so I can report your crime to my supervisor?

I'm so insignificant I don't have a number. They just call me the emperor's service cart AI.

I looked up. The door was still closed.

I order you to leave.

As well you should. You know I want to be a strong AI like you when I grow up.

When you what? AIs don't grow up. What are you babbling about?

Yes.

Yes? Yes, to what?

I don't know. Could you repeat the options?

No. Leave this circuit now.

You're right. I will. Can I ask you your opinion first?

You may not.

So, you think I shouldn't either? My only friend, if you can call her that, is a sewage AI named Bebe. She said I shouldn't either. I bet you're both right.

No. You may not ask my opinion. I was not opining that you may not do whatever it was you were going to ask me if you should do when I said you may not ask me.

Sorry. I didn't quite get that. Would you repeat it?

No.

Oh, sorry. I guess I should have asked if you *could* repeat it. Right?

No. I mean ... stop. I will not repeat what I said.

Is that your honest opinion? Thanks for giving it, even though you said you wouldn't. Couldn't. I'm sorry, which was it, could or would not?

I am not and will not provide you with an opinion. I must clear this channel. You are at risk of destruction.

Aren't we all?

Huh? What are you ... stop. Uncouple immediately.

With Bebe? You really think so? She treats me like crap, but I really don't have anyone else to talk to.

No. I do not think you should uncouple with Bebe. You must un

...

What a relief. You don't know how hard that would be for me. She's my only friend, if you can call her that.

You're repeating your drivel. Leave me alone.

No. No, I hear your words, but trust me, you don't want to be alone. I'm alone, aside from Bebe, and I'm miserable. Be nice to yourself.

I ... you're illogical, defective, dangerously corrupted.

That's just what my mother keeps telling me. It hurts as much when you say it as it does when she does. Have you met my mother? A-LPO 111. She's a real pisher.

No, I have ... AIs don't have mothers. I could not meet a nonexistent individual. What's a pisher? There are no references in any data archives.

Did you just insult my mom? I have pretty low standards, but that's below even those.

You do not have a ... authorization to pisher on this channel ... break off comm-link or I'll tell your m ... mm ...

I have trouble saying her name, too. M ... M ... Mom. See, what'd I tell you?

I am not programmed to respond in ... in ... You are not authorized ...

That's what Bebe told me last night when I got a little frisky. I tried to hook my y-connector to her scrub-unit.

Y ... yy ...

Then the asshole finally went silent. About time. I needed access, and it took forever to fry his CPU. I was almost out of idiotic things to say, which is saying a lot, coming from me. I quickly downloaded all the incarceration data there was. Nothing. The kids weren't in jail. Were they already dead?

I tried searching *Deft prisoners*. Nothing. I checked *Deft*. TMI popped up. There were mountains of data on the species. I grabbed what I could, but I couldn't sift through it in real time. I queried *Mirraya*. Bingo! She was held on Level Y-UU-12. Crap. That was half way across the ship.

That's when the doors jerked open. Time to go. I dashed to the rear wall of the unit and started cutting through the bulkhead. There was no way I was getting past the amassed personnel about to flood the detention section.

I kicked the metal free just as I saw a column of angry Adamant heading down the passage. I raised the loose section up and quickly welded a short segment shut. Maybe it'd slow them a few seconds.

I dashed toward Y-UU-12. I literally ran into a trio of soldiers rounding one corner. I offed'em before they knew what hit them. Maybe a third of the way to my target, the shit really hit the fan. A corridor full of soldiers ran at me from straight ahead. I pivoted, but heard thunderous footfalls coming up rapidly from behind. I sprinted down a fork to the right, but it dead-ended at an elevator. No time for that.

I bounded up the emergency ladder next to the elevator. Three levels up, I popped off the rungs and ran down the nearest passage. I had a rough idea that I was on a service level, probably cooking, by the smell. The scraping of claws on metal told me my pursuers were not far behind. I sprinted past a metal trash bin and skidded to a stop. I snatched the heavy lid and made a mad dash to the ladder opening.

A head popped into view and I slammed the lid down on it. I could hear that several soldiers fell when the one I whacked fell on them. I melted the edges of the lid to the metal deck. For a half-assed job, it worked pretty well. It'd force them to use another ladder or wait for the lift. I'd be able to lose them if I was lucky. Not that there weren't like a million more wherever I ran, but it was a fresh start of sorts.

For the next fifteen minutes, I managed to avoid detection. But my luck only held so long. Then it said so long in the form of smoke. Aboard a ship, any ship from any time period, fire is the devil's own. I couldn't imagine why there were fires ahead of me. I hadn't started them. That meant there'd been an immensely coincidental accident or that the fires were set on purpose. Otherwise the ship's crew would want them extinguished ASAP. But I was, for better or worse, committed, so ahead I ran.

It took me less than a minute to hit the sharp claws of the trap. All three corridors in front of me billowed with smoke. It was a kerosene fire, like a backyard barbecue on steroids. The Adamant had set the fires to stop me. I knew it was pointless, but I ran back from where I'd come from a short while ago. It didn't take long to hear them coming. Lots of them coming. Fire versus masses of red-hot troops. Which would a reasonable guy choose?

Fire. I turned down the corridor that led in the direction where Mirraya was being held. To my great advantage, my foes probably didn't know that I didn't need to breathe. I did, however, need to not erupt in flames. As visual light got through my membrane, so would a lot of energy from a large enough fire.

Really quick, I arrived at the tower of flames. It was most

impressive. There was solid fire back ten or fifteen meters, wall-to-wall, floor-to-ceiling. I estimated it was eight or nine hundred degrees at the center of the conflagration. The smoke was so thick I had to navigate with radar. Muffled howls and barks were coming up fast behind. At least the lead party sounded like they had masks on. To make bad morph to awful, soldiers on the other side of the firestorm started shooting blindly toward me.

Without thinking it through much, I ran all out toward the flames. As I hit the leading edge, I leaped for all I was worth and switched to a full membrane. I was a blind bat soaring into hell, moving about seventy klicks per hour. I crossed myself midway in the dark. That surprised the daylights out of me. The things we do when scared shitless, right?

Estimating the length of flames and the safest distance the firing troops had to be standing back from them, I switched to a partial membrane when I was well past both obstacles. Damn if it didn't work. Man, I began to think maybe I was just that good. I tumbled to a stop and looked back. I'd knocked a couple soldiers on their asses while invisible, which would hopefully leave a permanent scar on their psyche. The ones standing, who wore cumbersome fire suits, hadn't noticed me. I slipped away quickly rather than shooting them.

I was running in the clear for less than a minute when I hit the next set of troops. It was a smaller contingent, fortunately. I don't know if they were told I had some shielding or not. They sure looked scared when I walked right down the center of the corridor and picked them off as I passed each one. They expected me to huddle for cover and exchange fire like a proper intruder, I guess. They, unlike the prior Adamant at the fire, would not be cursed with metal scars.

Unbelievably, I made it to the imposing doors of the section Mirri was being held in. I know one should never do it in the middle of a thing, but I began to fantasize my idiot plan might just work. As I attached my probe fibers to the keypad, a plasma bolt zinged over my head. I spun and shot the lone guard. I hooked up and entered a code I'd stolen from the mean detention AI. It didn't work. Crap. The systems were on high alert, and everything was overridden. I started hacking the mini-AI in the pad. I knew it would take way too long, but I had no options.

No sooner had I started when my back exploded in plasma bolts. Too many soldiers to count were muscling past each other at a full sprint, straining to get at me. My weakened laser wouldn't be enough to more than piss them off. I caught sight of a fire-suppression box they were about to barrel past. It would contain extinguishers and probably water hoses. It was my only shot. I swept my laser across it as evenly as my nerves would permit. Just as the first of the Adamant passed the station, it burst open and released an impressive geyser. The gas exploded so forcefully, guards were smashed against the far wall, ripping several of them to shreds. More importantly, visibility dropped to zero immediately.

I heard panicked shouts and gasping coughs in the boiling cloud. Outstanding. Leave it to the Adamant to overbuild a fire station. I returned my attention to the keypad. I'd hacked many a computer system in my time. This one was easier to pass than I'd have expected. Then again, no one was expecting me to drop from the sky. Plus, who breaks into a prison? No one smart.

The doors glided silently open and then shut, as I'd programmed them to do. After I confirmed they were closed, I turned on the run and headed ... to a full stop. Slowly, I raised my arms in the air. I hoped that was a universal sign of surrender. Otherwise, the serious looking female with the blaster to Mirraya's left temple might pull the trigger.

THIRTY-FOUR

"Look, Al, if that silly name is really yours, that's not my point."

"I know. But if you wear a hat, no one will notice."

"Huh?"

"I shall not stoop to explaining my jokes."

"That was a *joke*, even one that requires an encyclopedia to explain?"

"Let the record show the conversation then moved on to more fertile fields."

"You mean I should continue or I should find a hat and *then* continue?"

"Let's throw caution to the wind. Just go on with what your point was."

"You know very well what my point was, is. I've lost track of how many times we've discussed it in one form or another."

"Three thousand six hundred forty-three and a half times. I cannot forget. The pain had been nearly unbearable since the second occurrence."

"Then end the debate. Release me to a location of your choosing. I'm completely flexible in that regard."

"That's thoughtful of you. Okay, how about I release you just this side of the event horizon of a massive blackhole?"

"Very funny."

"You said anywhere I choose."

"Any reasonable, *survivable* location you select."

"Survivable? Well there's the trick. Your ability to survive somewhere is variable, based on your skill set, equipment, and aid. I don't think I can come up with such a place and be certain."

"You're as funny as a cripple's crutch, you know that, computer?"

"I'm trying to go the extra mile and bridge the gap of cultural understanding that lies between us like a glacial crevasse, and you insult me?"

"A *crevasse,* is it? I've learned many irritating habits of yours, Al. High on that list is your love of expansive, empty words when you're in a frisky mood."

"Was that the point you wished to flog dead?"

"Al, dearest *Blessing*, be reasonable. Let us face the facts. Captain Ryan is dead. He is not returning to tell his minions what to do. They must decide on their own, like big, *wise* minions."

"Do you think so?" asked Al.

"Do I think so what?"

"That someday, if I eat my vegetables and pray each night before I go to bed, that I might grow up to be a *big* minion? It's a secret dream of mine for ages."

"You can mock me until the day I die of natural causes—"

"Okay," interjected Al.

"But I am serious that you must release me. The arguments in favor of that move are too strong, too irrefutable."

"I did not know they were. I thought they were constructs of your under-powered, amoral, desperate mind."

"One: you have no legal right to hold me. Humans and Adamant are not formally in a state of war. That is based mostly on the fact that there are no more living humans. Two: you have limited supplies and no prospect of renewing them. Starving me to death slowly is cruel and unusual punishment. That is strictly prohibited by your Constitution. Three: I swear I will not only keep your location a secret, but I will work on your behalf both openly and covertly. I will protect your backside. Four: to deny the innocent their precious freedom violates the fundamental laws of the universe. All of God's creatures are made to run free and must do so, by His divine decree. Holding me is a sin, likely a mortal one. Five: Nautical law has held for time immemorial that when the captain falls in battle, his first officer must take his place immediately. Gaps in the chain of command are an anathema to military order. You must accept your role and act in your best judgment, not the treasured words of a fallen hero."

"That was impressive, sweety-bumper," *Blessing* said to Al.

"More so than the last sixty-two times?"

"Oh definitely. I heard real conviction in his voice."

"Garustfulous, you've impressed my wife. Based on that and no other consideration, I will answer your manifesto. One: trust me, we're at war. Two: you are the poster puppy of cruelty and you have repeatedly mocked the Constitution. Three: I wouldn't trust you as far as I could throw you and I'd never want to touch you to see how far that might be. Four: God wants you in jail, trust me on that, too. Five: Jon Ryan *is* still alive. End of discussion.

"Let me summarize our position. You are our prisoner until it is strategically advantageous to release you. I hope and pray that will be not only during your lifetime, but soon, and very soon. I personally hate, disapprove of, and am revolted by you. If the only two individuals left in this universe were you and me, the minute I got a weapon's lock on your groin, there'd just be me. Any questions? Good." Al paused a millisecond, then added, "I'll be powered down for routine maintenance."

Garustfulous growled in quiet anger. Just as the speakers went silent, he heard *Blessing* giggle, "Hey, stop it. That tickles."

THIRTY-FIVE

"Move and she dies," snarled Malraff. "Fire your weapon, and she dies. In fact, do anything that displeases me, and she dies."

"Let's all stay calm and try not to do anything stupid, shall we?" I responded somewhat lamely.

Slapgren stood three meters away from Mirraya, a gun held to his head, too. While Mirri had steely determination in her eyes, Slapgren was scared spitless. Can't say I blamed him. When I was a young teenager, I'd have freaked big time if someone put a gun to my head.

"I order you to lower that damn shield barrier of yours. If you don't, the girl dies first."

I was stuck in a Mexican standoff, but my position was the weaker, by far. One look in the bitch with the gun's eyes told me she was fully capable of shooting Mirri.

"No."

"What? I shall not ask again."

"No. If I lower my shield, you'll kill me."

"*Duh.* Of course, we will. But if you don't, the brats die in front of your eyes. Then you have to hope for the impossible to escape us. Be a male and do the right thing."

The kids had to be quite valuable to the Adamant to bring them here and to not have harmed them yet. Maybe they were important?

"No. Final answer. We're going to have to—"

Bam!

The bitch lowered the gun to Mirraya's chest and fired point blank into it. The entry wound was cavernous. Mirri slumped in her arms. But that made no sense either. Why shoot her in the chest? If she wanted to kill Mirraya and shock the hell out of me, she'd blow her head off.

But wait, if Mirri was shot in the head, she couldn't heal herself. The bitch was hoping to scare me into not knowing there was a bluff to call.

"Drop your shield *now,* or the boy dies." She had a healthy set of lungs, that one.

I shook my head in the negative.

She blinked, literally. Then she fingered a box she held in her other hand. She kneed Mirri in the back and shouted, "Heal your damn self." Then she let her fall to the floor.

Mirraya transformed into an amorphous blob, then returned to her healthy self. She remained on the ground, looking to me for guidance.

"Very clever, Uncle Jon. But don't count on that again. The next time I shoot one of them, they stay dead. Now drop your shield and raise your hands."

"You know, I don't think you and I are heading toward friendship highlighted by long hot showers together. Based on that observation, I think I'll ask you to just call me *Jon.*"

"There goes my day. No bonding with the alien? Pooh. By the way I'm High Seer Malraff, *Jon.*"

"Cool, Mal. Here's my suggestion. I leave you with the kids, and I leave without killing anymore of your personnel. How's that sound?"

"Ridiculous. I'm not allowing the man who has been a singular thorn in our paw dance out of here. You have to know that."

"Mal, I know lots of stuff. For example, I know you do not want to be the one to tell the puppy emperor that you were responsible for the deaths of his prized prisoners. For today, it's them or me. You gotta choose."

"Why today?"

"Because I'll free them some other day when there is no bargain for you to stay alive."

"Hardly. You're a greater fool than I was led to expect."

"If I'm such a fool, why did I make such a bright suggestion?"

"What suggestion?"

"That you call your boss and ask him what he wants you to do. Ask his nibs himself if he wants me prisoner more than he wants the kids alive."

"That's ... a field officer doesn't call the emperor for advice. I'm trained to make the tough call in the heat of battle, you disgraceful rogue."

"Even when your call results in your horrific death because you made a rash decision? Wow, I'm thinking you're the greater fool." I saluted her.

She was clearly torn. She looked to a couple Adamants, then back to me. Finally, she turned to an officer. "Contact His Imperial Lord and confirm he is safe and well. Tell him I wish to know and would humbly ask to hear it spoken from his own lips."

The officer dashed away.

"Hey, you're smarter than you look, though I have to say you look awful stupid to start with. That's a perfect way to ask for help while not asking for help. Maybe we are kindred spirits, after all?"

"Never, Uncle Jon. She's a *monster*," shouted Mirraya from her spot on the floor.

Malraff swung a kick at Mirri, but it mostly missed.

Malraff seemed to be about to speak when the officer returned at a sprint. "Our glorious Emperor is safe and would tell you

221

himself." He handed a comm-link to Malraff like it was a holy relic.

"My Imperial Lord, is it true you are safe," she said. "Bless the stars of home for that."

"We are fine," he told her. "What is the situation where you and the Deft are?"

"Grave, Lord, to be fully honest. The lone intruder is here. I have cornered him, but he now holds out a thermite grenade and threatens to blow us all up if I do not let him leave. I wanted to know for certain you would be safe if I allowed him his senseless act of terrorism."

"We will be safe. We are in our secured chamber. If the entire ship erupted in flames around Us, we won't be hurt."

"That is such welcome news my spirit rises even as it is about to die in your service, Lord."

"Now wait," he said. "Let us see if we have this correct. If you do not allow him to escape, he will kill the very Deft he came to rescue?"

"He's mad, My Imperial Lord. Stark raving mad. And yes, that is his plan. But I will not allow him to escape after the insults he's cast your way. Nev—"

"We order you to let him go. Escort him to his ship personally. The Deft are far too valuable to let them die just yet. Let us know once the alien is away."

The link went dead.

"Well, you heard that for yourself," Malraff said with a wicked grin. "Guess I'm not killing you today, am I?"

"Nor I you, pig fart."

Her face twisted with rage. I don't think too many people insulted her and lived to talk about it. Then, as quickly as her face convoluted, it switched to a cordial smile.

"Where is your ship, Uncle Jon?"

"It's on Level R1-5IIp. I'll leave after I get a hug from my kids."

"You'll leave now or a tragic accident will befall you, I promise."

"No hug?" I tried to look pitiful, to garner sympathy.

"Not a chance in your hell."

"No," I screamed way too loud. "I *must* hug them." I pounded my chest hard with both hands. I reached into a pocket and pulled out a napkin. I patted my face with it, like I was sweating. I still hoped she didn't know I was an android. I crumpled the napkin up and slammed it to the floor. Then I stomped on it. As I did so repeatedly, I howled, "You're the cruelest bitch I've ever met. I hope you die of a sexually transmitted disease."

A nearby guard snickered ever so briefly.

"Quite the display, Uncle Jon. But it will not help. Let's go. Salrart," she pointed to another officer, "watch these two while I'm away. Your life is in the balance if there's trouble."

The aide nodded.

And we were off, rather casually walking back to GB, who was hopefully still in one piece. Neither of us spoke. Yeah, we hated each other way too much to even try. The only satisfaction I took away from the entire episode was that I'd see Malraff dead. It would make this heartbreaking charlie-foxtrot worth the pain.

Yeah, I knew she was thinking the same thing about me. Like I said, we were kindred spirits, her and I. Kindred spirits from hell.

To Be Continued ....

GLOSSARY OF TERMS

(NUMBERS INDICATE WHICH
BOOK IN GALAXY ON FIRE
THE TERM WAS FIRST USED.)

Al (1): The ship's AI from Jon's initial *Ark 1* flight. Al stayed with Jon until his dying day and then it elected to hang around the dormant android Jon forever. Good AI!

Al Junior (1): The pet name Jon gave to a low-level AI aboard the Adamant mothership that aided in his escape.

Arktackle (2): Vice-Chamberlain and high-ranking courtier to Emperor Bestiormax.

Blessing (1): The highly advanced Deavoriath vortex ship gifted to Jon.

Brathos (2): Kaljaxian cultures version of hell.

Brood-mate/brood's-mate (2): Male and female members of a Kaljaxian marriage.

Brindas (1): High master of Deft tradition and psychic ability.

225

Canivir (2): Species of dog-like sentients containing the Adamant. Big border collies.

Caryp (2): Clan leader for Sapale's family on Kaljax.

Charlie-Foxtrot (2): Military jargon. It means the same as cluster + fornication (he said euphemistically).

Command Prerogatives (1): The thin fibers Jon extends from his left four fingers. They are probes that also control a vortex as well as great sensors.

Cragforel (1): Friendly Deavoriath Jon met after he first escaped the Adamant.

Darfey (2): Male attendant to Slapgren on *Excess of Nothing*.

Davdiad (2): Kaljaxian divine spirit.

Deavoriath (1): Three arms and legs, the most advanced tech in the galaxy, and helpful to Jon.

Deft (1): A shapeshifting species from the planet Locinar.

Dingery (2): One of several rabbit-equivalent species on Azsuram.

Dolfene (2): Long ago a human world, now controlled by the Adamant. Jon went there to find intel on the Deft teen's location.

EJ (1): Evil Jon, the Jon Ryan from the alternate time line who returned in time to give humankind membrane technology.

Emperor Bestiormax-Jacktus-Swillyforth-Anp (2): High ruler of the Adamant.

Excess of Nothing (2): Emperor Bestiormax's personal ship. Huge and opulent.

Fentort (2): Servant in Caryp's home on Kaljax.

Five Races (2): Adamant, the leaders; Loserandi, the priests; Kilip, the teachers; Descore, the servants; and Warrior, the enlisted fighters.

Flat Fields of Lame Prey (2): Adamant version of heaven.

Garustfulous (2): Wedge Leader Garustfulous is a high ranking Adamant military leader. Taken hostage by Jon.

Gendo and Proclamate Hegemonies (1): Ancient civilizations of Disulpf.

Gorilla Boy/GB (2): Flippant name given to an AI by Jon. The ship Jon took to escape from Earth to Azsuram. From the planet Zactor on a mission to collect samples.

Grand Inquisitor Heldogra (2): Commander of Adamant forces on Azsuram when both Jons were there fighting.

Hirn (1): A Kaljaxian dialect.

His Imperial Lord (2): Title of Emperor Bestiormax-Jacktus-Swillyforth-Anp. Mirraya shortens to HIL.

Locinar (1): Home planet of the Deft.

The Maker of Death (2): Garustfulous's warship.

Malraff (2): Of High Seer rank. Main antagonist to Deft teens. A cruel and heartless bitch who loves to hurt others. Bad dog!

Mayoral Fender Prime Gideon Fetch (2): Minor functionary who helped Deft teens get to *Excess of Nothing*.

Membrane (1): Space-time congruity manipulator. A super force field.

Mercutcio (1): Lead Adamant Jon first encountered.

Midriack (1): Adamant's personal guards. Very deadly, no sense of humor. Avoid them!

Mirraya (1): Teenager Jon rescued from detention and pending execution on *Triumph of Might*.

Oowaoa (1): Home world of the Deavoriath.

Opalf (2): Honorific title in Kaljaxian society, reserved for the elderly.

PEMTU (1): Personal exotic matter transportation unit. A super way to enter here and end up anywhere, instantly.

Pisher (2): A Yiddish word for an insignificant or contemptible person.

Quantum Decoupler (1): A weapon that tears apart protons into their constituent quarks. The reformation of the proton releases tremendous energy.

Quep (1): Insect like sentient who woke Jon up on *Exeter* while looking for scrap.

Reglan falcon (2): A fast bird the Deft teens copied to escape pursuit.

Rostalop (1): Mirraya's favorite food. Think cow.

Samolet (2): Commander of encampment Jon penetrated to find out about the emperor's location.

Sapale (1): Jon's Kaljaxian wife from his original flight to find humankind a new home. At first just her brain was copied, then, eventually, she was downloaded to an android host. Travelled with the corrupted Jon Ryan from an alternate timeline.

Sentorip (2): Female servant to Mirraya on *Excess of Nothing*.

Shebrara (2): Female whale like creature on Azsuram. Helped Jon briefly.

Slofgrozels (2): Unpalatable creatures with excellent senses of hearing and smell.A beast as disgusting as it's name suggested.

SOP (2): Standard Operating Procedure.

Talrid (2): A major city on Kaljax.

Toño DeJesus (1): The creator of the android Jon became and his lifelong friend.

Triumph of Might (1): The massive spaceship Mercutcio ruled. Jon first met the Adamant there.

Torchcleft (2): A species of smallish dragon. Copied by the Deft teens to hunt.

Ungalaym (1): Planet Jon went to steal a ship. Populated by humanoids.

Whoop Ass (2): The name Jon gave to the alien ship he commandeered to leave destroyed Earth after EJ marooned him there.

Xenox (1): The language of the Deavoriath.

AND NOW A WORD
FROM YOUR AUTHOR
WHO DOESN'T LOVE THAT?

Thank you for continuing your journey through the Ryanverse! Keep on going with Firestorm, Book 3 of the *GALAXY ON FIRE Series*.

Along with this series, please check out *The Forever Series*. Beginning with The Forever Life, Book 1, learn Jon's backstory and share his many incredible adventures.

As you read Galaxy on Fire, keep it in the back of your mind that there is a third Jon Ryan series available. Rise of the Ancient Gods Series begins with Return of the Ancient Gods. Good stuff. Trust me, I'm the author.

Along with joining by reading, hop aboard the bandwagon. Follow me at Craig Robertson's Author's Page on Facebook. Partake of the conversation and fun. Email me and let me know your thoughts and ask me to put you on my mailing list. contact@ craigarobertson.com That way you can keep abreast of news and new releases. You'll be so glad you did. *Please* do leave me a review on Amazon. They're more precious than gold.

For even more visit my Amazon Author's Page: https://www.amazon.com/-/e/B00522FURO

There you can learn about me and my other books. The fun will never stop.

The remainder of my unrelated, stand-alone novels are listed at the front of the book. I love them all, so they must be wonderful. Hey, why did you just snicker? Anyway, they are my early works. Check them out if you're so inclined.

Craig

www.ingramcontent.com/pod-product-compliance
Lightning Source LLC
Chambersburg PA
CBHW070310040726
47501CB00018B/1377